OTHER BOOKS BY
GEORGE FETHERLING

FICTION

The File on Arthur Moss
Jericho
Tales of Two Cities
Walt Whitman's Secret

POETRY

Rites of Alienation
The Dreams of Ancient Peoples
Selected Poems
Madagascar
Singer, An Elegy
Plans Deranged by Time

LIFE WRITING

Travels by Night: A Memoir
The Writing Life: Journals 1975-2005

THE CARPENTER
FROM MONTREAL

Author's Note:
Set in a demimonde that existed long ago, this novel contains speakers who use language that was common in their generation though it would make us wince if heard today. Fictional characters, however, must be allowed to have their own voices; that's one of the ways we hope they might begin to stir and perhaps come to life for a few moments.

The following is a work of fiction. Many of the locations are real, although not necessarily as portrayed, but all characters and events are fictional and any resemblance to actual events or people, living or dead, is purely coincidental.

The Carpenter from Montreal could not have been written without the help of the Woodcock Fund, the Access Copyright Foundation, and these individuals: Maya Assouad, Bruce McDougall, Merrill Fearon, and Frank Mackey. It is dedicated to my friend Jeanne Finstein.

Cover design by Debbie Geltner
Book design by WildElement.ca

Library and Archives Canada Cataloguing in Publication

Fetherling, George, 1949-, author
    The carpenter from Montreal / George Fetherling.

 Issued in print and electronic formats.
ISBN 978-1-988130-47-7 (softcover).--ISBN 978-1-988130-48-4 (EPUB).--
ISBN 978-1-988130-49-1 (Kindle).--ISBN 978-1-988130-50-7 (PDF)
    I. Title.
PS8561.E834C37 2017   C813'.54   C2017-902040-4
                                                       C2017-902041-2

Printed and bound in Canada.

The publisher gratefully acknowledges the support of the Government of Canada through the Canada Council for the Arts and the Canada Book Fund.

Linda Leith Publishing
Montreal
www.lindaleith.com

THE CARPENTER FROM MONTREAL

a novel

GEORGE FETHERLING

PROLOGUE

The muzzle flash was so beautiful, like the explosion of a bright five-pointed star, that it tempted the triggerman to continue firing a few seconds longer than necessary. But he was a professional, controlled, *réservé*, even *timide*, and did not allow himself to linger or be distracted. The racket, the yellow petals of pulsating light, the screams of the woman inside the expensive automobile, the man dead on the pavement—it was all part of a single event. It was three hours past midnight, three hours past New Year's Eve 1937, and snow was coming down like ashes after a fire.

Cynthia McConnell:

I've been away.

But now I return to the city, though not to the city as it used to be. Like so many of them, it has decayed and is dirty and dotted with monuments to the heavy industry that no longer exists. It's not much of an exaggeration to say that it's a ghost town, though I realize that you might find it odd that I'm the one saying this.

If I myself was in any way complicit in the collapse, I plead absence, though I admit to being at least associated with it, but distantly. After Father died, and with Mother incapacitated and overseas, my brother took control of the family business. Eventually he had to merge it with a bigger one, and we ended up with thousands fewer workers of our own. Then, in a few years' time, the amalgamated company was put up for sale just when the contract with the most powerful union was about to be renegotiated. You see, the union became angrier the more blood it lost. Both sides were so weak that my brother gave in to demands that the workers have the right to say yea or nay on any proposed sale. There were two offers, one from Europe and the other from South America. Everybody chose the wrong one. The new owners folded

9

up the whole operation when it couldn't make any profit paying American wages.

What used to be the McConnell plants didn't need to remain vacant long before turning a rusty brown. During my family's long reign, some steel was made from scratch, so to speak, and other steel was made from scrap steel. The mills themselves became scrap for somebody else to buy and melt down. Before long, downtown began to follow suit while slums such as the Triangle became even more evidently what they always had been. I suddenly find myself thinking these odd words: "The sins of the fingers are visited upon the toes."

When I was growing up, nothing struck me as odd. That's how innocent (or naive, distracted, indifferent or isolated) I was. It never occurred to me to ask why people named McConnell, only four generations at most from what was no doubt some kind of thatched hut in Scotland, should be Episcopalians rather than Presbyterians. (The answer, for any younger people who might be hearing this one day, is simple: we made a fortune and so graduated to "the high church"—a term with a double meaning.)

I was never a popular girl, not a leader, not the one with the perfect figure and the perfect friends, but neither was I an outcast at school. I had fun yet I was prone to a kind of melancholy, as though I were somehow remembering a different sort of life than the only one I actually knew, in fact knew far too well for my liking. Before I started at the Academy, when I was still at the Country Day School, where we were beginning to study Latin and boys, subjects equally indecipherable, a small band of us would visit the cemeteries and eat prepared sack-lunches there. I remember once going to the Catholic cemetery on a lark, eating whatever Hedy had prepared for me, and then wandering about, reading the names and dates of all those poor people from Ireland and all those sad Italians. The frolic turned to sorrow and I had to keep the others from seeing my tears by hiding behind a sort of cenotaph for the departed Humility of Mary sisters. There was a Jewish cemetery as well, but I never even knew of its existence when I was growing up.

Mostly we went to *our* cemetery, as Father, and probably my brother too, called it. My final home was like a vast spread-out city, with orderly streets and lanes, a living city for the dead, located in what has become just the opposite, a dead city for the few who still persist or insist on living here. Neatly kept-up little dollhouses of granite or some lesser stone, a community of many thousands of smug Protestants, some of whom, to use an expression I once heard Pete say, "died standing pat." Some more pat than others. We would giggle about great-grandfather's monument. Actually it was the family mausoleum but the statue of Old Pig Iron, as he used to be called, stood atop it. His marble self sported a lengthy beard and a frock coat. He was raising one arm as though to indicate Heaven or the direction in which the stock market should be heading. The mausoleum door is immediately below his feet. It has a tiny window, an iron-grilled one about the size of a sheet of typewriting paper, through which you can peer in at the creepy old caskets, including mine, supported by shelves on either side. There always used to be chipmunks playing nearby. No dogs allowed, you see, and plenty of mature oaks with acorns galore. Little white-tipped tails poking up everywhere. Life goes on. Somewhere. It is the same with humans.

Edwin Staffel:

The old City Hall and courthouse sat on the highest point of ground. Police headquarters were at ground level and the municipal jail was on the top floor. From several of the south-facing cells, the luckiest prisoners could glimpse a sliver of the town down below, while the warden, from his office, could see the whole spectacle. Steeples shot up from the jigsaw puzzle of streets and buildings that led down to the riverbank, where the McConnell steel mill spat out orange fire. One steeple belonged to St. Alphonsus Church, the second to St. Vladislaus, and the third to St. Michael's Cathedral: in order, the German-speaking Catholics; the Polacks; and the Irish and the greaseballs, as well as all the various other types of hunkies and miscellaneous souls who happened to be Catholic. Catlicks, as many pronounced it. St. Al's was right downtown, not far from St. Mike's, while St. Vlad's, the poor parish, was just the other side of the High Level Bridge. Beyond the bridge, almost hidden from even the jailer's view, was the Triangle. The area was called that because the first few north-south streets nearest the water mimicked the river's course, breaking up the straight line of the original grid. They met in a point with the railroad right-of-way and the streetcar tracks coming down from the other side, making a shape like a piece of pie.

The Triangle grew up around the old Seventh Ward Market. Farmers from all the surrounding counties once brought their produce and animals there on Fridays, and starting at dawn on Saturdays the place would draw the chefs from restaurants and big hotels such as the Congress, not to mention those from the hospitals and the asylum, followed by the general public, shoulder to shoulder until day's end. With money in their pockets the freeholders and stockmen would stay over another night or maybe two to sample some city living. In the square around the market house and some of the nearby streets, which were long and dimly lit, were giant saloons where pistachio shells littered the floor. Small sometimes unnamed hotels far outnumbered feed stores. Two short streets away was the Line, which was not much more than a wide alley with high curbs, with crude little two-storey houses, several of them with red bulbs screwed into the overhead porch light sockets.

Once Prohibition was brought in, a year and a bit after the end of the war, far fewer farmers came to town—the last of the old harness-makers had closed his shop—but more and more thrill-seekers were arriving in private automobiles, shopping for pleasure in the blind pigs that kept changing their names every few months, or else never had names to begin with. Cafés like the Paddock. These were cafés where you couldn't get a cup of coffee but that's what they were called. Everyone knew who owned them but the people whose joints they were admitted nothing. Deeds and tax records always indicated ownership by someone else, sometimes even by those whose legal residence, truth be told, was Holy Cross Cemetery or one of its competitors. Living or dead, those who controlled these places, and who skimmed cash every night, never left a trace. They got the idea from the cops.

Be patient now, I'm allowed to be long-winded when I tell you what came about. Let me talk. Then you can ask questions. Let's get this done before I turn into just one more dead old man.

Allan Ostermeyer:

If Staffel will permit, I can, in my capacity as the *nisi prius* lawyer I used to be, speak to you *ad antiquo* and indeed *ab initio*—all the way back to the beginning.

For as long as anyone could remember with any degree of exactness, one of the city's most vivid examples of a healthy democracy had been the way that, by some tacit agreement worked up who knows how long ago, a Democrat and a Republican took turns being police chief, an official appointed by the mayor. Mayors were usually re-elected as a reward for good conduct or longevity but nobody broke with the bad idea of alternating chiefs even if it meant giving the job to the other party. In essence, the same two chiefs would take turns until one of them died. If the dead chief had a grown son or a brother (in one case, an uncle) who needed a job, then the post stayed in the family. If no survivor could keep the tradition alive, the city's worthies met in a solemn and highly secret session in the mayor's office or the locked billiard room of the Parthenon Club and chose someone to step in. Twice in fifty years or so a new surname joined the orderly procession of history, creating a new line of dominoes on the game board, yet without reversing the foreordained outcome. Continuity not only made sure there were jobs-for-the-boys, it was the true lifeblood of good government. You had to have been baptized and confirmed in the right parish and brought up in the right ward and recommended by your alderman to get work picking up the city's garbage or get hold of a part-time position shelving books in the Carnegie Library. Exceptions might be made only when tumultuous events in the outside world shook the city's foundations.

Cynthia McConnell:

I don't know how—I'm not even certain why—but I find myself back downtown sometimes. There is no travelling involved. Rather, I simply appear without any effort on my part and even without the slightest wish to be there. Some force must be controlling me. Call it what you will. I am inside the experience without being part of it.

You might say that it is rather like being cast in a movie but being stuck behind the screen on which it is being projected. No one in the audience can see me, and I take no part in the action in which I am nonetheless—well, participating. In all, I have made probably thousands of these return visits, though I say this without being capable of making sense any longer of just what numbers mean.

Most of the people I see are new people, new to me and, at least as compared to me, new to the life of the world and the world of life. They are the still-living who would not have known me had we been contemporaries, would not even have heard of me were it not for that night in the Caroline Apartments and the events surrounding it. And yet time is wavy, and on occasion I may glimpse a familiar figure, or perhaps only a familiar face on a different body, and then I am filled with a sense of astonishing menace. That's when I fear a return of the genuine threat to my safety, though this is absurd as of course I am no longer alive. I used to believe, as many do, that dreams are small hints of what time might be like after one has stopped existing. Well, the reverse, it turns out, is just as true. I look down, I look about; I look through doors and walls; I float above the pavements and rooftops. In the morning when you're brushing your teeth or fixing your hair, you look into the mirror but don't see me on the other side staring at you and imploring you to join me.

Allan Ostermeyer:

In the course of a long career, a lawyer hears many things he knows aren't true and learns truths that he cannot reveal. That was the part of the notarial life I always found frustrating and uncomfortable. I can clearly recall what I'm about to speak of, but I warn you that it is not easy to substantiate, at least not to evidentiary standards.

When Herman Clouse was growing up, there were three newspapers published in English every day, and another in German. A year or two after graduation from the parish high school, with top marks, a medal for English composition, and a small cash prize for General Business Practice, Clouse was trying hard to find a place in journalism. Everyone turned him away at least three times. But serial rejection was simply another proof of his determination. He began to spend his spare time, a commodity that anyone without a job possesses in abundance, at a saloon, the sort that was old fashioned even then. It was the place where newspapermen, ones of all allegiances, mingled uneasily. The saloon was named the First National, as though it were a bank—which for some it was. Many of the reporters and desk-men cashed their pay there each week. This practice, as the owner knew, saved time, as much of the money would be spent there as well.

The characters who worked on the *Enterprise* were the most efficient of all, for their employer still made up the payroll in banknotes and specie, as in a mining camp, calculating each person's time card down to the minute and putting the folding money and silver into a small brown envelope, to be picked up and signed for—twice—at the cashier's window in the lobby, near where readers came to take out subscriptions or place classified ads.

Young Clouse wasn't a drinker. He wasn't terribly social, though during periods of intense listening he could force a wide smile as a way of not appearing to eavesdrop. In this and other ways he heard details of stories reporters could never get into type, not to mention occasional gossip of newsroom vacancies, usually on account of death. Back in those days the papers still had tramp reporters, and tramp printers too, working their way, often quite willingly, from city to city, passing by for a moment on their way between birth and the grave. Clouse's ears were funnels through which information poured, and in time he got what he believed was the first brilliant idea in what turned out to be his one-idea career.

In a deal that I hardly need say was a scandal that lined the pockets of several men around town, resulting in a bluster of editorials pro and con, political cartoons galore, and the usual calls for Something To Be Done, the two traction franchises had been bought up and consolidated, creating a single city-wide streetcar line that would extend its rails into remote lands that the new owners, members of the Parthenon Club, had been buying up for a song from elderly farmers, and which they intended to develop as suburbs. Clouse went to the head man of the consolidated system and convinced him to give him free space in all the cars: little hooks on the walls, just below the cord a passenger tugs on to request a stop. The hooks would hold what Clouse called *The Rider*, "the world's smallest newspaper." It was one sheet folded and cut into four pocket-size pages and set in tiny type. It was full of little bits of local news picked up here and there as well as snappy sayings and jokes, a few in German or Yiddish dialect. Most of all, *The Rider* had a good deal of carefully paraphrased loose talk crying out to be overheard in the humming commotion at the First National and other joints. It took only a few weeks for passengers to spread the word about the new publication. Some even sent in hearsay of their own. Eventually, Clouse was able to sell a few business-card ads, such as one for the Waiting Room, a café located at the downtown loop where the east-west cars, the No. 17 and the No. 31 especially, turned around and headed back the other way, ferrying workers to their jobs or returning after most businesses had closed. It was an especially busy place on cold or wet days, when you could kill time there until your car waddled into view, ringing its tinny-sounding bell.

The first time Clouse was served with a writ of libel, a lawyer named Karl Metzger called on him, offering to take the case pro bono and putting his mind at ease. Metzger's name was vaguely familiar as a member of the somewhat secretive gang of anti-McConnell politicians and fixers who, while strangely little known as a group, were powerful persons in the city. One small illustration of their leverage and drag was the fact that, once Metzger became involved, the threat of a lawsuit turned out to be only that, a threat, and vanished in a puff, which probably kept others' grievances against *The Rider* from boiling over.

In what was perhaps another manifestation of Metzger's cultivation of him, Clouse was later offered a position as a reporter, not on the more enterprising *Enterprise* but on the city's historic but third-place paper, the *Inter-Ocean*. There he showed a remarkable aptitude for learning and retaining everything about everybody and about all the components of publishing, from the business office to the composing room, from the pressmen to the boys hawking papers on downtown street corners. The more knowledge of whatever kind he acquired, the more he sensed others were careful in his presence. So he was eventually able to move over to the *Enterprise*. He believed the change was based solely on his own merit.

Karl V. Metzger Esq. Attorney-at-Law could not sense impending earthquakes the way certain animals are said to do. Still, he was gifted in seeing subtle tensions deep within the landscape and dramatic swings in the civic equivalent of barometric pressure. In his case the coming catastrophes were political. Months after Europe barged into war in August 1914, the newspapers began to fill with alarming stories about German troops hoisting Belgian babies aloft on their bayonets. Hatred began to build, and like most hatred was stupid beyond redemption; sauerkraut disappeared from menus, Bundt cakes vanished from bakery shelves. Metzger could see how his enemies and those of others like them would use prejudice as a serious weapon indeed.

In May 1915, when a U-boat sank the liner *Lusitania*, people he knew began adopting less German-sounding versions of their names, a useful halfway measure. The following year, when calls for America to enter the war would eventually drown out the voice of isolationism, many took the art of prudence to the point of clairvoyance, thanks to the help of the friendly Judge Wingerter. For example, the judge granted a man named Kasper Vossen a change of name. Kasper Vossen became Casper Fossen, de-Teutonizing the forename and spelling the surname the way it was pronounced; later, Fossen was given leave to become Cecil Foster instead. A man with a name like that, why he could manage a Ford automobile dealership or sell insurance—or have any other position of trust. No Belgian babies would be harmed.

By the time America did get into the conflict in Europe in 1917, the nation was in a state of high war fever, which is to say anti-German hysteria was even worse than earlier. Anyone with roots in Bavaria or Prussia was retroactively becoming Swiss, Alsatian, or Dutch. German ceased being taught in the public classrooms and finally even in the St. Alphonsus parish school. Anti-German agitation, bordering on riots in their intensity and scope, erupted. At one stage, a band of men hustled German-language books out of the Carnegie Library and fed them to a bonfire.

One day, Metzger telephoned Clouse (whose own name could have been worse—*Klaus* or *Klause*) and invited him to lunch at the Parthenon Club. As he went about his reporting assignments, Clouse had often hurried by the place, noting the bronze plaque that read *Members Only*. (I had myself been a guest there but there were no members who were Jews.) He went through the huge double doors with oval panels of bevelled glass, checked his hat in the cloakroom and identified himself as Mr. Metzger's luncheon guest to the concierge sort of fellow standing behind a well-oiled wooden counter. He was directed to the club room where the day's papers, national as well as local, hung from wooden rods, and men sat in chairs upholstered in green leather.

Clouse and Metzger chatted briefly about business conditions in the town and the mood at City Hall. Clouse was two years shy of thirty, making him eight years Metzger's junior, but he felt that the gap was somehow wider than that.

In the dining room, the steel magnate McConnell, the successor to Pig Iron McConnell, who had established the family fortune with government contracts during the Civil War, was seated at a corner table with his son. McConnell Junior was a decade younger than Clouse, yet Clouse didn't have the younger man's calm entitlement, for he hadn't the money to back it up.

The waiter, a Negro, recited the day's menu. Clouse made his selection, Metzger wrote it down along with his own and signed the paper, putting the bill on his account. By the time they were working on the main course, Metzger (who thought he'd have a go at the trout today) was full of praise for Clouse (lamb). It occurred to Clouse that Metzger was about to offer to put him up for membership. But the proposition, when it came, was vastly more important and even more unimaginable.

"You know the legal position of the *Staats-Zeitung*," Metzger said. "Old Eichelburger, the nominal publisher, is only the resident manager. The beneficial owners are his uncle and some other members of the family who live in the old country; that is, not even American residents much less citizens. If the business were to be seized as enemy property, as I believe might be possible, I wonder whether you would care to take it over as editor and publisher." Clouse tried to keep his eyebrows in place. Metzger continued: "I am confident that I could raise the capital from"—he discreetly looked around the room, not in McConnell's direction—"investors who aren't comfortable with the *Register*'s stand on things. They'd underwrite a plan for turning the old German rag into a successful English paper. That would certainly stir things up a bit and in the longer view might be quite lucrative."

Clouse wasn't certain he agreed with the last point. "The circulation has been declining for at least a generation, maybe two," he said. "Frankly, I'm surprised the thing still comes out at all. Excuse my language, but it's so goddamned anemic. Some retail advertising, Friebertshauser's Famous Sausage Shop and such places, and rarely any national linage at all. They're still using that old single-width Duplex press. Prints, what? A ten- or fourteen-page paper?" As he scoffed, he suddenly realized that he might appear to be talking himself out of a job. He dredged up a few words from his shallow well of wit.

"There does, however, seem to be a roaring trade in classifieds thanking St. Jude for his intervention."

Metzger smiled. "Those are all good reasons to imagine that, even without the war, the concern would be unlikely to go for much at auction. I would add to the list the fact that their old building, while downtown, is quite small and has not been well cared for. And I am given to understand that the presses, were they to be sold separately instead, would attract interest only from dealers in scrap."

No one would ever call Clouse stupid. He understood perfectly well what was being offered and why.

"Our group," Metzger went on, "feels there is enough business for the *Register*, the *Enterprise*, and whatever we decide to call this new one. As for the *Inter-Ocean*..." Metzger allowed his sentence to trail off, suggesting that the paper in question would sooner or later cease to exist.

"What would you wish me to do?" Clouse asked.

"To meet with us at length and draw up a plan for how you would invigorate—one cannot honestly say *re*-invigorate—the paper both as its editor and as the managing partner. Make no mistake, you'll be in for the scrape of your life. But you're a fighter. You're the only new blood in journalism in this city." Metzger smiled with wily warmth. "Those are two of the reasons you have so many friends."

There was a moment of pensive silence, so Metzger went on. "People know how much you've learned and they know you've got ideas. You're clearly the sort of fellow who must be given his head. We see it like this: we would

float a new company and give you a twenty per cent interest on the understanding that you would draw no more
cash at first than you do from your present job, but would
see a big return over time, in proportion to your level of
success. The remaining stock would be held by the rest
of the group, though with some extra shares coming to
me for brokering the arrangements, which I don't believe
will be too terribly complicated if we move decisively."

Metzger saw that his language sounded vague and
overly optimistic. "The federal government, you know.
Or you can imagine. Believe me, that part won't be easy.
Still and all, this is the moment to strike." He smiled in
self-mockery. "The peace, if it comes sooner than expected, could put the kibosh on the whole deal." Then he
looked his luncheon companion straight in the eye. "*Bis
Sie etwas anderes sonst von hören, bleibt es unser Geheimnis.*"

"*Ich verstehe,*" Clouse replied.

Even people who didn't know German would have
been able to understand the tone. Keep this to yourself
until you hear from me.

Cynthia McConnell:

Am I trying to deal with a crisis I left behind? I have no
idea.

For some reason I find myself carrying a gallon of
paint. I move without any effort whatsoever past the ruins
of places I once knew or must have known. All types of

businesses, many of them vacant if not yet abandoned but with their fate spelled out clearly. I am startled to be reminded of the past by many of the signboards and by the names in dust-covered directories in the lobbies of office buildings: Rinehart, Nieswonger, Schamp, Heilmeier, Schellhause, Imhoff. (I knew Barbara Imhoff in school. She was so thin as to appear almost two-dimensional. She had long legs and little more bust than a boy. How I envied her retrospectively in the days when I embarrassed myself by trying to impersonate a silly flapper.)

To my surprise, I spot Ed Staffel, that ancient busybody and collector of tall tales and inventor of yarns. He used to know Pete—and everyone else in town, at least to hear him tell it. I am surprised that he has not yet come over to the dead side—at least I don't think he has—but instead is standing right there with his back against what used to be the old German drugstore, *Apotheke* slowly fading away above the doorway. (Is this why I am carrying a can of paint?) His moustache is going white, but he is otherwise much as he was back then. Or am I having a dream? I wasn't aware that I am capable of dreaming. He moves away slowly but in a jerky fashion, like a fish startled in an aquarium, and as he does so my own spirit wanders, meanders.

Edwin Staffel:

Let me tell you about Jim Joseph. First of all, that wasn't the moniker he was born with. It was Lahoud. His name first appeared in the *State Journal*, as the old *Staats-Zeitung* had become, in 1921. Although it was a common name in the Lebanese area down in the Triangle, it was neverthe-less misspelled that day in the police blotter column, one of the most widely read features in the paper. Wedged in among the routine list of gamblers, leggers, and bartend-ers charged with minor liquor transgressions was "Fouad (Jimmie) Lahood, 22, no address given."

Even at his young age, the fact that Joseph had elud-ed publication for so long was remarkable to those who knew what went on in the city after dark, or who liked to pretend they did. They chuckled that the name Lahood—the hoodlum—also described the person's profession, like a character in a morality play. Clouse, who always seemed to be everywhere at once, chanced to see the spelling cor-rection that the man in the slot sent to the composing room in the overhead pneumatic tube for the second edi-tion. He asked the slot man who had written the story.

The man on the rim dodged the question. Everyone knew that Clouse was given to flying off the handle at errors in spelling and grammar, a habit they put down to his not being a college man. He had once fired a kid for writing that someone "rented" a taxi rather than "hired" one. "I am prepared to wager, Mr. Clouse, that the error originates with the officer who filed the green sheet with the sergeant, for the police in their haste are often care-less." Clouse harrumphed as he walked away.

In the years since then, Joseph had become known to simply everybody. He lived for gambling, especially on the ponies. Hence the name of the joint he ran: the Pad-dock Club. People who happened to have briefly caught sight of him even one time bragged of being acquainted with him, and those who were in fact slight acquaintanc-es boasted of their deep bond of friendship. Lahoud was already a subject for harried clergymen seeking a last-minute topic for denunciatory sermons on such sins as the racetrack. Most of the businessmen in the city, the ones who warmed themselves on wintry days by the big fireplaces at the Parthenon Club and were kept cool dur-ing hot spells by its slow teak-bladed fans, were similarly disparaging, loudly so if also hypocritically. They secretly admired Joseph because he evidently had amassed a great deal of money in a short period, having begun without any at all, born in an alley in the Triangle, in a grim little two-storey structure that housed three families, though it seemed scarcely large enough for one of normal size.

Unlike the greaseballs, the Polacks and all the other hunkies, the Lebanese fleeing their Ottoman oppressors did not usually seek jobs in McConnell's steel mill or in the foundries, plants, factories and other shops whose whistles sent thousands of men in their work clothes and cloth caps shuffling along the streets three times each day whenever the shift changed. The Greeks, and the Turks, with whom they maintained a reciprocal hatred, accused the Lebanese of trying to high-hat the Europeans. The truth was they gravitated to that at which they excelled, but at which they did not necessarily prosper. They kept small grocery stores, local bakeries, tiny tailor shops and an uncountable number of strange Lebanese coffee houses where men sat all day drinking strong coffee from minuscule white cups and playing endless hands of bastra.

Abraham Lahoud and his wife Marianna had immigrated to America in 1898. One child died of crib fever, and another was carried away by no illness that could be identified. Abraham himself was taken by the influenza epidemic and left no estate, for he had been a mere clerk working behind the counter in the shop of one Mr. Jalad whose place sold staples such as olives and lamb and functioned as a confectionary that did a land-office business at Easter and Christmas and of course every August on the approach to the Feast of the Assumption of the Blessed Virgin.

To preserve her stability as best she could, the widow fell back on the only two resources she had left: her remaining son and her church. Like virtually all the Lebanese in town, the Lahouds were Maronite Catholics who belonged to Our Lady of Lebanon. Contrary to local practice, the church had no steeple, only an unadorned flat roof, for the building was meant to suggest the squarish architecture of the old country. The whole congregation, families such as the Khourys, the Saseens, and the Amends, came to Mrs. Lahoud's aid, for everybody knew that in difficult times one could never depend on those they called "the Americans." But Jim took the surname

Joseph, for he knew he had to become one of the Americans to prosper as they did. He understood them. He was clever, and he had skills: one was for arithmetic. Another was for fixing automobiles. In retrospect, these were seen as the sure signs of the gambler and the bootlegger.

Before he won what became the Paddock Club in a marathon poker game one night, Jim Joseph worked at C. & J. Livery. For years, Culver & Jones was a stable that looked after not the horses used by the big breweries and bakeries, which had extensive stables of their own, but those of icemen and junkmen. Mr. Culver, on in years and the last of his line, had entered the automobile age half-heartedly and late in the day. He owned three Ford taxis and one big truck, a five-tonner, I believe, all acquired second hand. Culver would paper over the C. & J. emblem on the front doors, cover the taxi light on the roof, and rent the autos to local undertakers to fill gaps in a cortège. Joseph got his city chauffeur's permit so he could drive one of the hacks when he wasn't working on the engines. Either way, there wasn't much business.

Jim Joseph was courting a young woman named Zelfa Nassif. Zelfa (the name sounds Turkish to me) was six years younger than Joseph but even so was considered someone who might one day exceed the usual age for Lebanese girls to marry. They had met at church. Jim was enough of a Lebanese to know the rituals. He could not be alone in her company. When he called at her family's home, he had to sit with her in the front room with her uncle, who had a mean look and a suspicious nature. She was covered in dark clothing. The conversation was stilted. At other times, usually on Sunday afternoons, they were permitted to stroll together or, on other days, to attend social events sponsored by Our Lady. On those occasions, they were chaperoned by Zelfa's much older brother, Peter.

Peter Nassif, as a precaution, had changed his name to Pete Sells when America went to war (and he with it). His father's brother, who had thrown somebody's tarboosh over the ship's rail as the immigrant ship neared New York to symbolize how he felt about the Ottoman Empire, had advised Pete to take a new name before he joined the army. He feared that the boy might be sent to fight against the Turks: "The first thing they do is cut off the manhood of any Lebanese boy they make prisoner." Pete, however, got sent to France. In later years, people would say, if only to themselves, that he was one of those who had been wounded on the inside rather than the outside.

Zelfa's brother was a strongly built fellow with a lively manner and dark complexion (he could be mistaken for a Greek). Jim Joseph and he were somewhat alike, one foot in the Lebanese culture but the other most definitely not, even when it irked them to be so divided. They were eager to make their way in the world, and speculated how they might do so as a pair. They liked each other. Pete, as his friend requested, made a special appointment with his uncle so that, with what was hoped would be the unanimous approval of the family, an outcome that he had been engineering behind the scenes, Joseph would formally ask for Zelfa's hand.

One day a local Greek, someone known to be a gambler and loan shark, appeared at the garage, asking about hiring the truck but only if Joseph were the driver. In Culver's absence, for the old man was quite ill by this time, Joseph listened to the bargain being proposed. The Greek didn't give the impression of being careless with money, far from it, but for six or seven days' use of the truck he was offering more than the heap could ever be sold for.

"I need you to pick up a shipment of goods in Montreal and drop it off to me here," the Greek said. He lowered his voice and handed Joseph a note. "Here's the address," he whispered. "It's the Carpenter's place. You won't have any trouble." Sensing that he was sounding too mysterious, the stranger said: "It's an investment of mine. It's a valuable shipment and I need somebody reliable." Reluctant as he was to get involved with a Greek, the bridegroom was inclined to accept, at least after discussing the idea with his brother-in-law.

"Better a Greek than a Turk," Pete said, and that decided it.

The upward journey to Montreal, while not without incident, was quite pleasant. Finding his way through the unfamiliar city to a nondescript warehouse in an outlying industrial area in the eastern part of town was more complicated. There wasn't time to absorb much information about his surroundings. Joseph watched as a crew stacked a full load onto the truck bed. The crates contained unmarked bottles of alcohol protected by straw. The men hardly spoke to him.

The return trip was quite different. Jim drove east all the way to Sherbrooke and then beyond, until he came to the place where Quebec touches the top of New Hampshire. He parked out of sight at a crossroads and checked to see that the tarpaulins were secured as tightly as possible. Then he went into a combination diner and gasoline station where everybody seemed to be jabbering in French under an electric sign that read *Gaz* and ordered the blue-plate special. After a couple hours' sleep in the cab, he drove to the border crossing. The customs post was deserted, closed for the night just as he had been told it would be. He steered southwest across Vermont and into New York State. From then on the trip was a breeze. It earned him four hundred dollars, so he figured the Greek probably made at least four or five grand clear profit.

A few weeks later, there was a second trip, this time with a different pickup point in Montreal and a different route home, crossing into Maine before turning back east and then south. The likelihood of a third gave Jim the jitters. As a gambler by temperament and avocation if not yet by profession, he could sense when a cycle of good luck was about to begin or end. The Greek may have been blessed with the same instincts, for he didn't return.

Jim Joseph and Pete Sells, boys with all-American names, conferred like seasoned American businessmen. Jim had a store of cash surplus to his immediate expenses and Pete had a certain small amount of savings. Jim proposed that they ante up all they had so that, with the addition of evenly spaced promissory notes, they could buy

C. & J. from Culver—maybe a long shot, but maybe not, considering that Culver was more or less retired, in fact if not in name, and that his enterprise was withering.

"Here's what I think we should do," Jim said. "You run the taxis. We'd have three medallions, so let's make use of them. Grease as many bartenders, bouncers, redcaps, and hotel porters as you can to get them to call our fleet." He felt silly referring to the trio of badly beat-up Fords as a fleet. "I mean, promise to grease them until we get some cash running through this place. Nurses in the emergency rooms too. You get the idea." Pete smiled to show that indeed he did. Jim nodded toward the truck. "Meanwhile, I'm going to rebuild that."

Pete had joined the army voluntarily (Jim was never called up) but though he was very strong and talkative— he was a mouthy fellow actually—he seemed to shrink and kept his trap closed tight whenever somebody mentioned the war. Whatever had happened to him in France during the war seemed to split him into two pieces—the normal man the family knew, and a wild one, very unpredictable. Wild with sorrow? With bad memories? Jim would say years later that he had heard Pete speak about the war only one time. Something about coming upon a group of men who had been dead for quite a while, but the tank watches on their wrists were still ticking away.

Pete wasn't one for attending reunions or joining organizations. He was more one for stepping out for an evening, a long evening. Loud as he could be at times, nobody even saw any evidence that he was a drunkard, but he had something in common with the many who were. He'd go on a bat around town for two days and two nights, usually with some throb hanging on his arm—and not always the same one everybody had seen him with the previous time.

Allan Ostermeyer:

Hardware stores couldn't keep coils of copper tubing in stock, because so many were distilling liquor in their cellars or attics and selling it to the Joseph-Sells combination. What they produced fit in surprisingly well with the other hooch, most of it also of uncertain ancestry, purchased from bigger fish in bigger cities. Buying bottled stuff was expensive. But the profits were always large, sometimes nutty large, because America, the whole damn country, was a drinker's market. As for the local product, even if the quality was poor at times, Jim was happy to meet the demand and, in the process, bind the customers to him as their benefactor, a zany local boy who'd made good, someone they could respect. Pretty soon neither the stuff he brought in nor the stuff mixed and stirred in kitchens and in the back rooms of ma-and-pa stores, even when added together, could slake the city's thirst.

There was a big increase in business, and in profit, when Joseph and Pete acquired a floor of a vacant warehouse. The building had once been part of a brewery, which, like breweries all across America, had gone dark.

At the retail end, the Joseph-Sells partnership soon had more than thirty cabs delivering bottled goods to homes and offices round the city, always careful to ask for the fare shown on the meter in order to keep up appearances. The drivers were liveried, and looked so respectable that they even got some legitimate customers—usually someone new to town, some fellow who didn't realize what was under the floorboards and hidden behind a false panel in the luggage compartment. Often such passengers were headed to or from the train station. In one case, a C. & J. driver raced to Passavant Hospital with a woman who was about to give birth. That story rated a human-interest item on the front page in McConnell's *Register*.

The brothers-in-law were getting rich in a hurry, but Pete's money seemed to go out the back door as soon as it came in through the front. Not wanting their paths to diverge too much, Jim persuaded Pete to go in with him in a second joint in the Triangle, slightly bigger than the Paddock. It was a former billiard hall and lunchroom that Joseph suggested they tactfully rename the Café of the Allies, for the streets were full of patriotic veterans. They laid out considerable mulch, as they put it, to fortify the spot without giving it the forbidding appearance of the bunker it actually was. The renovations were done by workmen from out of town, from places such as Youngstown and Detroit, who didn't know one another and in many cases didn't even speak the same language. They worked without blueprints, so there wouldn't be plans on file anywhere. Ornate wood panels in the doors at street level disguised the fact that the cores were inch-thick steel. Up above, other doors, invisible ones, led to secret gambling rooms and still others, likelier looking, opened on plain brick walls. The best protection of all, though, was the fact that most of those who lived within a two- or three-block radius of the Allies were either relatives of Joseph's or Pete's, or friends of one of their families, or at least members of Our Lady of Lebanon.

Other than the Allies, though, Pete spent his dough on other things, using it up to paint the town, and to seduce women. And he was a big one for automobiles, the faster and flashier the better. He graduated from an early Hup-mobile coupe with booze in the rumble to a 1925 four-door Nash touring car to a '29 DeSoto before going all out, eventually, just as everything seemed to be collapsing, on a red '30 Duesenberg Model J, the fastest thing on the road. Wherever he parked it—sometimes he couldn't remember where he'd left it the night before—kids would gather round, touching it and making up senseless little songs about it.

Edwin Staffel:

This story I'm telling now is the story of how, over time, the two men had four specially modified tank trunks with internal bladders of booze floating inside a cargo of, let us say, milk—which is what the border agents or prohibition officers would find when they probed the tanks with dipsticks. One truck was actually painted with the name, address and telephone number ("Mingo 2150") of a non-existent dairy. One of the others purported to be the vehicle of an equally fictitious purveyor of coal oil. Demand was such that imports remained an important means of supplying the speaks and dives that sprang up on virtually every corner, pretending to be something else. Pete and Jim's only serious rival in the local business was the group associated with a man called Szabo, some kind of Hungarian, most likely, though many believed he was simply a frontman for the Greeks.

"That hunky plays rough," Pete told Joseph. Szabo's goons slapped and kicked bartenders, smashed furniture and shattered plate-glass windows to instill in their victims a preference for Szabo's own brands of beer and booze. "Why don't you let me take the fight to their backyard?"

There was something about Pete that many—some Anglo-Saxons and some others—found disturbing. This quality, whatever it was, had helped him become, certainly in his own view at least and probably for real, the chief muscleman in town. By comparison, Jim, who was lighter-skinned, was soft spoken and struck folks as being by far the more educated of the two, though both men had quit public school and set out to learn the street. But Jim was the strategist and the tactician.

Pete kept returning to his idea of fighting the competition, but Jim finally put his foot down. "I know that would give you satisfaction. But we'll win everyone back with better stuff and slightly lower prices. No tough act."

Pete looked skeptical. "As I see it, there's two things we oughta do: cut out the competition we've got and put a scare in anyone else who'd want to take us on."

Jim answered in what he hoped was exactly the right tone of voice. "Pete," he said, "don't burn down the town."

The *Register* and the *State Journal* didn't agree on much. Both papers, however, ran similar columns each Sunday. The feature in the *State Journal* was called NEWS OF COLORED FOLK and contained such small items as appeared throughout the paper when white people were involved: notices of births, engagements, weddings, not to mention bake sales and other events benefitting the black high school, the Negro Knights of Pythias, the Elks Lodge No. 26 (the Booker T. Washington Branch), and the Abyssinian Baptist Church. People of African descent made it to page one if they committed violent crimes, for journalistic segregation didn't apply to crime stories, which all readers loved, or death notices in the obituaries, which were paid advertising.

For example, under the headline BULLETS FLY AT CUT RATE CAFÉ was the tale of a man and woman "wounded by pistol bullets in an incident at the notorious Cut Rate Café, known to police as a speakeasy." One Henry Denton ("colored, 50, of no fixed address") and Evelyn Cook ("colored, 31, of 1034 rear Lewis-street") had been treated for bullet wounds. The shooting was described as concerning the liquor traffic. It was a minor incident but for Joseph probably a telling one, as it showed that everyone—people he'd never heard of, and he'd come to know just about everyone—was trying to make a killing in the business even when they had no capital and no connections. That's when, as I understand it, Jim Joseph phoned the *Register* and asked to be put through to Mr. McConnell.

"It's probably better if we don't meet here."

"What about at one of the mills?"

"No, that presents the same difficulty. Why not come round to the house? Say Tuesday, mid-morning?"

"That's swell," Joseph replied, though he usually got out of bed at noon.

"You know the house?"

"Everyone knows it."

The Negro housekeeper who opened the door was expecting him. She was elderly, pleasant but somewhat formal. "Mr. McConnell asks you wait for him in his study."

The house was so large that she had to lead him to the room. The structure had been built by McConnell's grandfather, the one called Pig Iron. With partners, he and others had put up an iron works and foundry, but McConnell eventually bought out the others and got control of a bank. His son then parlayed the whole kit into two big steel mills. During the war in Europe, following Pig Iron's own road to initial success, the grandson made scandalous profits on government contracts. Now, even with the war having recently become history except in the minds of those who fought in it, the family business was set to enrich yet another generation. The boom was going full blast.

The den had a huge desk—mahogany, Joseph thought—with a brass lamp and a shade made of green glass. Various fountain pens were lined up perfectly on the immaculate blotter. On two of the walls hung framed paintings of horses and racing scenes. Along the third wall were glass-fronted bookcases. On the fourth, a collection of antique pistols was displayed. In a few moments, a teenaged girl entered the room. She introduced herself as Cynthia McConnell. "Daddy wanted me to tell you that he will be down in a few moments. Please let me know if there is anything you need in the meantime. Would you care for a drink?" She felt a bit awkward asking that, as she wasn't of drinking age. "If you would like something to eat, I'll ask Hedy to get it for you. No? Well it's a pleasure meeting you, Mr. Joseph." With that she withdrew in a mist of youthful charm. What a well-brought-up girl, he thought, albeit one who must have hated growing up in such an old-fashioned monster of a house.

McConnell offered Joseph a chair before taking his usual place behind the desk. "I've long wanted to have a chat with you," he said. "Sometimes it seems that everyone else in the city is a Republican, as my father, his father, and all their friends were. That's why I purchased the *Register*. I thought there should be another voice, a liberal voice. Don't get me wrong. I'm not a red sympathizer." He smiled without quite chuckling. "I admire the way you've used your brains and recognized circumstances that allow you to make money."

"I have a partner, my brother in-law."

"He enjoys explosions, does he not?"

"I don't know that that's exactly"—he started to say "true"—but at the last moment ended with "the case."

They both knew what McConnell was talking about. A recent story in the *State Journal* had been headed, DYNA-MITING SAID 'REVENGE' FOR TIPS GIVEN DRY AGENTS. The report wasn't very well written. It began:

> The nature of the explosion which blew away a section of the wall at the home of Albert Mousa at 1012 Quincy Street early yesterday morning, and a motive for an attempt to demolish the home and injure the occupants, have been found by city police investigators, it was announced late last night.

Police had found paper fragments at the scene, the remnants of the parchment wrapping of a dynamite stick, suggesting the weapon of choice. The likely motive was revenge for "tipping off" Prohibition agents as to the existence of a whiskey distilling set-up. No one had been harmed, but the explosion was of a bigger league.

"This is spinning out of control all too quickly," McConnell said. "There'll be blood if this continues. In just the past little while you had that case of some legger gunned down leaving a pool room. You remember? When the police searched the body they found a large amount of cash in his pockets. He was wearing a diamond ring. He was from Youngstown or some place."

The public wouldn't learn of these things if the press didn't print the stories, Joseph thought to himself. "The damn *State Journal* plays this stuff to the hilt," he said.

"So do all the papers, including mine, and the radio as well," McConnell replied. "We, you and I, have to find a way of, shall we say, reducing the danger—and the bloodshed."

"You sound like you have an idea you want to let me in on."

McConnell's mouth made a discreet little smile. "There's nothing to be done about the federal people. These drys are on a crazy jag. It's fuelled, as far as I can see, by moral indignation and the desire for quick promotion. The best route is to stay away from them—and have them stay away from you as they search for bigger fish elsewhere, and for more publicity. The locals, they're the ones you can control to a surprising degree."

"You have an interesting mind," Jim said. "And interests that I can see are rare in a man of your—position."

McConnell opened a drawer under his desk and extracted two glasses and a bottle. "This is the real McCoy. Scotch from Scotland, brought over right after the war. Nothing added and nothing taken away, made by men whose trade it's been for generations. In short, this isn't the stuff that your joints sell to the workers of McConnell Steel."

Jim nodded thanks. "They're the core of my business," he said. "There must be, what, six or seven thousand of them hitting the pavement when their shift ends. Every noontime and every midnight they're out there in their work clothes, looking for a drink and maybe a game of chance. And that goes for the seven o'clock shift too."

"I see that you are a man who understands the steel industry," McConnell replied. "But flatter me by assuming that I know a little something about your own line of work as well. You've got to diversify. You need money coming in from different sources. The only way to do that in this town is to get into politics."

McConnell went on. "It's long been my ambition to throw our moron of a mayor out of office. And to elect a substitute who will replace the righteous martinet of a police chief. Once you've done that, you can set up a system for sharing some of the wealth with the force. Then you can do anything, lucratively but quietly, and let the Washington sorts, most of whom are as crooked as a dog's hind leg, forget about you—if the amount is right."

McConnell was on to something. As Jim Joseph took his leave of the steel magnate, he was already thinking how he might proceed.

From the diary of Cynthia McConnell, submitted into evidence:

This has been a very uneventful day. Also a very uneventful year, so far. Daddy is tied up in business. He always is. He doesn't have time to give me the sort of affection he gives his son. I wouldn't tell anyone that, but there's no use in lying to myself, is there? Mother has been sick again, mostly from drinking I guess, but not as bad as she would have us think. I went down to the kitchen to ask Hedy to make me a sandwich. She was listening to a concert of sacred songs on the radio. I don't care for such music at all. I suppose I am a heathen but I'm not really sure. But as I love Hedy, I love to see her enjoying what she likes. I have been trying to get up the nerve to ask her about boys, as I certainly can't discuss such things with Mother. But Hedy is really old. Nobody seems to know exactly how old. I know she would listen to me and offer advice, though I'm not sure boys weren't different when she was my age or even if she remembers them.

Allan Ostermeyer:

If history is the judge, then my role is simply that of an *amicus curiae*—a friend of the court. In this capacity, permit me to file a brief on a young cop named Nolte.

Nolte had heard all about the Eighth Street Shuffle, which sounded like a new dance craze but wasn't. The shuffle was a legitimate policing technique, or so said some of the boys at headquarters, at least the roundsmen. The idea, developed and refined during the first two or three years of Prohibition, was that the officer directing traffic at Eighth and Commerce, the centre of the universe, would wait until the intersection was chock-a-block full of people who had just stepped off the curbstone and had gone only a couple of yards. Then, suddenly, the copper directing traffic would blow his whistle and motion broadly with one white-gloved hand so that the pent-up auto traffic would start moving into the crowd. Folks would scatter, running to get out of the way of the drivers honking. Anybody running with one hand inside the sleeve-hole of his coat was probably packing a pistol. That was the idea. The shuffle was a little trick for telling the bad guys from the good, for at a distance you couldn't always distinguish one from the other.

Oh, what the hell, Nolte thought. On all four corners, the people were five and six deep. The shoppers and diners had been let out of their offices at noontime. He gave a shrill blast on his silver whistle, stuck up his palm and gestured. Suddenly the traffic that had been idling wasn't idle any longer. One woman picked up her young child and made for the safety of the sidewalk over by the big clock that glowered from its cast-iron pole outside Himmelrick's Jewellers. Other people scurried this way or that; one man lost his hat. Sure enough, one fellow came huffing along at a fast trot and holding his right mitt firmly in his left armpit. He was wearing a navy-blue overcoat, and Nolte studied him for a few seconds. He looked like a pug-ugly all right, a well-decked-out pug-ugly. Nolte nabbed him on the sidewalk and patted him down right there outside the Congress Hotel, which was maybe where the jasper was headed, though he wasn't carrying a bag. And no surprise, but to Nolte's secret delight, the guy had a banger in a shoulder rig. On the other side he had a fat billfold with the stub of a train ticket. He'd come over from Youngstown. He had New York State identification, and an old draft card showing he was IV-F.

46

Despite being relatively new to the force (he had joined in December 1923 or January '24), Nolte knew what to do. He prodded the joker along to the nearest call-box and used his key to open it. The sergeant at the other end of the line said to bring him in right away. "Turn the signal back on," he said. "You don't have to wait for a man to relieve you." Meanwhile the guy from New York or wherever was mumbling to himself. "Goddamn hick burg. This ain't supposed to happen. I was wearing my lucky gun."

The sergeant hadn't sounded mad on the phone, but he sure was when was Nolte brought in his prisoner. The shuffle has no place in this department, the sergeant said; you're putting innocent citizens at risk, and so on. Granted, that was true, but Nolte couldn't see what the change of tone was all about. After all, the big tub of lard was being charged with carrying a concealed weapon and possession of an unregistered weapon dangerous to the public. Sarge gave Nolte a long speech, before waxing po-etic about forgiving the sins of youth. "Consider yourself lucky that you already got past probation."

Sarge knew the kind of grief he would be letting him-self in for if he tangled with the city police board that the mayor ran. But he didn't know if Nolte knew. He would reassign him to a beat next month somewhere where there was nothing to do but patrol a schoolyard during recess. Back in law school we might have called this a DBE: *de bene esse* ("for all the good it might do").

Edwin Staffel:

City Hall was an imposing place of reddish stone with a high, square tower at one end, and rows of tall windows with rounded tops. On the roof loomed a copper-sheathed dome that time had tinted peppermint green. Atop the dome stood a statue of Blind Justice. She was supposed to hold the Scales of Justice breast-high in her left hand but they had broken off around 1885, struck by lightning, some people swore. The result was that Justice was left holding one fist in mid-air. She looked as though she were punching somebody or shooting craps, or possibly just ordering a drink or hailing a cab. Upstairs, over the police department, up the curving staircase with its wide marble steps worn down by decades of soles, its oak banisters polished by generations of grubby mitts, were the various offices, the courtrooms and the council chamber, and above that the jail.

From his office on the fifth floor of the Board of Trade Building, the lawyer who represented Harry Szabo in his various business enterprises had witnessed the incident outside the Congress Hotel and knew instantly what was taking place. He immediately called the chief and also the bondsman. He thought he had better tell Szabo too but knew better than to say anything important to him over the phone. In any case, Szabo, with his rudimentary English, was much easier to understand face to face.

Clustered around St. Alphonsus up the street were little places selling Bibles, prayer books, and various other religious articles. In the same spirit, lawyers like Oster-meyer and bail bondsmen and even a few private detectives did business almost in the shadow of City Hall. One of these bondsmen was busy in the police headquarters only a few moments after the sergeant finished lecturing Nolte. The out-of-town tune-up man never even saw the inside of the holding cells downstairs, because he was freed before he could be booked. There was even some thought of giving him back his gun, but appearances prevailed.

Jim Joseph was thinking it might be time to get away for a while, for Pete was driving him bats. Pete had seemed all right when he was acting as the go-between in getting Zelfa to marry him. And he had been okay when the two men first started working in the legitimate taxi business; he didn't appear to have such a hair trigger back then. But he was a thug and a dandy besides, slicking back his hair and parting it in the middle, wearing pleated trousers with a zip fly, and always making a show of the fat bankroll in his pocket—and it wasn't a Michigan bankroll either. He had taken to hand-tailored suits, hand-made shoes, and pearl spats. Often of an evening he could even be seen escorting an onyx walking-stick with a gold knob of a handle. One time he beat a man with it. Maybe he'd always had a violent side but had covered it up—I don't know—but there was no way of predicting his temper. Pete had a big itch he kept scratching. Sure, he had fallen into his half of all this easy dough and it showed. But Jim wondered whether this development, coming so soon after the war, might one day cause Pete's personality to burst like a bad appendix. The war Over There had become the war within. Which was the chicken and which the egg? No one could say, certainly not me, not at this late date. I'm just another newshound living out his days.

There was no one Jim could confide his feelings to. He certainly couldn't talk to Zelfa about her brother's problem any more than he could discuss business with her. Although she too was getting used to luxury (she was fond of fur stoles, complete with the foxes' little snouts), she was a devout young woman. Proper. She usually went to church alone, but on those occasions when the two of them went in the car, she sat in the rear seat while he sat at the wheel. Only flappers and prostitutes did otherwise.

Jim thought it might be time for him to maybe go to Canada and see if he couldn't buy a load of that stuff himself. He wondered how others had managed to do as well as they had up there and wanted to see the place for himself: insurance. He packed a two-suiter and told Zelfa he wouldn't be gone long. He had no sooner left town than he began worrying what sort of harm Pete might inflict on their enterprises when he was the only one in charge. But there it was; there was nothing to be done.

Jim got to Montreal and checked into the Queens Hotel first, but then moved to the Windsor, with its marble staircase and big cupola. The place took up one entire city block. From the Windsor he went to the address of his second pick-up spot and asked around for the Carpenter, but no one would talk, even after he gave his bona fides.

He persisted. Finally a tall man brushed him off more deliberately: "*Y a personne qui peut le rencontrer.*" The words came out in a whisper, though there was nobody near enough to overhear. Even without knowing the language, Jim got the drift. All he could do was to write a note alluding guardedly to his business dealings with the mysterious Carpenter and leave his room number at the Windsor.

Without a car, he just began wandering. The city breathed money and coughed it too, discreetly, prudently, but unmistakably. Most everything about it was exciting, and all the rest was merely wonderful. St. Catherine Street made Commerce Street seem like a cowpath. The buildings were far taller, in both height and importance. And one just knew somehow that the stylish women passing on the sidewalks were wearing fine lace underneath. The crowds were so thick that they impeded the streetcars. There was a far greater profusion of different automobiles than he had expected, more cheap Fords of course but also more of everything else, going up the scale: Plymouths, Packards, DuPonts, Durants, Hudsons, LaFayettes—all of them honking constantly, day and night. He even saw some models that nobody back home had ever seen. He decided to stick around for a while.

Everything in Montreal pricked his imagination, even sights you wouldn't expect to affect him. One day, he went down to the market in Jacques Cartier Square. Block after block of farmers' trucks, four parallel rows of them, unloading their produce and animals. By comparison the old Seventh Ward Market in the Triangle was a roadside stall where old men peddled tomatoes. Every inch of Montreal seemed to crackle, as those who knew how to make all this money knew how to spend it just as easily, though with class and dignity. He went to the port, near the entrance to the Lachine Canal, and saw long snakes of railcars waiting to load or unload at the grain elevators.

Montreal was also a city of neon lit nightlife. Nightclubs were everywhere. It wasn't illegal in Canada to manufacture liquor, only to export it to the US directly. The Americans had to run it across the border themselves, though buyers and sellers would also rendezvous in boats and ships just beyond Canadian waters. And everybody who was in the know had heard about the islands south of Newfoundland named St. Pierre and Miquelon, territories of France. A Montreal family had built big warehouses there and had become phenomenally wealthy. They made a few extra bucks by letting American leggers and gunmen hide out there—those who were, as some would have said back home, making mutton.

One evening, Jim was in his room at the Windsor when knuckles rapped on the door. He figured it was a boy returning the suit he'd sent out for pressing. Instead, he opened the door to a big well-groomed man in his fifties wearing a camel-hair overcoat and a snap-brim fedora with an especially high crown. He would once have been very strong but now was just noticeably large. His hands were enormous. At a glance, a tailor probably would have pegged him as a forty-six tall, maybe even a forty-eight.

The visitor pointed his thumb at his own chest.

"Charpentier." He stepped inside. "You have been looking for me? I apologize for the long wait. To be frank, I was having people ask about you. It is a complicated process, yes?"

"I've got whiskey. Let me offer you a drink."

Charpentier's eyes quickly took an inventory of the room.

"No, thank you, please. But the next time you come to Montreal we will talk business before I"—he groped just a half-second for the right phrase—"give you a present of the town." He made an expansive gesture with his massive arms. "We are surrounded here by possibilities. Nothing is far away."

The Carpenter left as quickly as he'd come. Jim wondered whether the man had even been there at all.

Back home in their four-bedroom suite in the Rose Apartments, a high-toned residence that the less fortunate considered rather hoity-toity, Jim knew what to expect. Pete had telephoned him in Canada to say that Harry Szabo had acquired a bit of black stuff in his neck. The call had been brief. There was no reason to go into detail. Joseph hopped immediately on the overnight.

Zelfa was still sound asleep, lying across the bed diagonally, entangled in new satin sheets. She was prone to worry, so he left her there, had a shower-bath and shaved, took the pins out of a brand-new shirt, and chose a fresh suit from the chifforobe. When he called Aurora 2500 he didn't have to identify himself. The dispatchers, all of them, all three shifts, knew his voice from the first syllable. "City Hall," he said when the taxi came, before changing his mind. "Go back to the garage. It's a nice morning. I'll walk."

He strolled up Commerce Street from Second to Fourth, past Factory Economy Paint and Wallpaper, Lanos Coffee (the Greeks!), Streamline Grocery, Schenk's Furniture and Appliances. Then on to Sixth, taking his time, looking at both sides. The sun seemed especially bright all the way to Eighth toward Ninth. The hotels, banks and office buildings all suddenly seemed small potatoes compared to Montreal's. The German People's Bank (the people in question still called it that, though the old signage had come down), the Security Bank and Trust, the Dollar Savings and Loan, the Hotel Florence, the Board of Trade Tower and so on, until you stepped over some invisible line into the land of supper clubs and movie houses: the State, the Regal, the Bijou, the Grand and all the others, which at night made a little spectacle of electric signs.

At City Hall, the chief of police was waiting in his inner office. He'd been waiting for some time, along with a female stenographer. Jim came in, took a seat without being asked, and laid his hat on the desk.

"Mr. Joseph, if that is the name you prefer, let us begin." Clearly he was speaking with such absurd formality owing to the steno's presence. What an ass. "A Mr. Harry Szabo was shot the day before yesterday as he was about to get into one of the cars at the taxi stand outside Neidermeyer's News Depot where, according to the sales clerk on duty there, he had bought a copy of the *Daily Racing Form*. Mr. Szabo is currently unconscious in Passavant Hospital.

Do you possess any knowledge of these events?"

"Only what you've told me. I've been away."

"Where were you on the twelfth?"

"Up in Montreal. I was staying at the Windsor Hotel. You can check that out."

"We will do so. What was your business there?"

"Like you say: business."

"Can you be more specific, sir?"

"As you know, I'm in the transportation and café business. I was seeing certain people there about a business proposition."

"What people, Mr. Joseph?"

"You wouldn't know them."

"I would encourage you to be co-operative. A crime has been committed—a man has been seriously wounded by gunfire—and it's my job to determine the basic facts as far as it's possible for us to do so." The chief, a political hack if ever there was one, then took a slightly different tone—but only slightly. "I believe you are somewhat familiar with this process," he said.

"Yeah, every time someone spits in the sidewalk you drag me or my brother-in-law in here for one of these little palavers."

"No one's dragged you anywhere. You are here of your own volition in response to our request." He said the last word softly, which seemed out of character. The chief paused for a couple of beats. "You don't deny that you're in the liquor trade?"

"Everybody's in the liquor trade. You too, at the retail

end." Jim smiled.

The steno started to smile as well but caught herself in time. She thrust her face into her notepad.

"Are you personally acquainted with Mr. Szabo?"

"I may have seen him."

"What does he do for a living?"

"I have no idea. Why don't you ask him when he gets well?"

"Oh, we will. As soon as the doctors permit us to interview him. Until that time, do you deny that you and he are commercial rivals?"

"You're barking up the wrong tree. Sure, I serve liquor in my cafés. Some nights it flows like Niagara Falls. You should stop by. Please take this as a personal invitation. I can promise you'll be treated real swell."

When the chief answered with a devastating stare, Jim shifted gears. "Listen, right now the city's full of new faces and not all of them are here for my hospitality. Hell, the place has been overrun for weeks with goons from Youngstown and all sorts of other hot spots. Open your eyes if you want to know what's going on. Then we won't have to keep on having these"—he paused to show his contempt—"interviews."

"Joseph, you're far too modest. You have a great deal of power in this city. Why deny it?"

"I run nothing but my own business."

"By which you mean—what, precisely?"

"You know. The Paddock, the Allies. I got no reason to lie to you. That's how I make my living. And yes,

I like to gamble. It relaxes me. Some nights I win and some nights I lose. It makes you learn how to get along with others. You should do the same."

"Who do you suppose Szabo lost to, and over what?" The chief was laying it on a little thick. It was ridiculous. What a four-flusher.

Jim had the ability to look innocent or jovial when the situation called for either effect. He stood up, smiled pleasantly but not too broadly, and picked up his hat to go.

"I hope Mr. Szabo has a speedy recovery, as I'm sure he will." His hand shook the chief's hand despite the latter's reluctance to accept such a paw, and likewise with the young secretary, who would one day tell her grandkids about the encounter. He closed the door behind him. In an instant his silhouette was visible through the pane of frosted glass in the door. The silhouette moved on but his tread was still audible. He passed the elevator and walked down the corridor toward the bottom of the circular staircase that was spilling people out into the main lobby.

Jim picked up the morning papers and folded them under his arm. As he was passing the Congress Hotel, he dropped into the barber shop off the lobby, surprising George Taggart.

The name on George's birth certificate was Ernest, but even his wife Hedy called him George when they weren't alone together, though not without a sense of worn-out resignation. All Pullman porters, which is what Taggart had worked at when he was younger, were known as George. That way, white passengers could behave a little high-hattedly toward all porters anywhere, impressing sweethearts with the easily remembered generic forename and expecting big grins of gratitude when they doled out small gratuities.

Normally, George Taggart would be asked to stop around the Joseph apartment and collect almost every pair of shoes, returning them cleaned and shined the next day with all the laces replaced. You treat shoes like a fleet of taxis, Jim believed. If you're going to keep the greatest possible number of autos up and on the road at any given time, you need a schedule of when to change filters and fan belts even when they don't obviously seem to need replacing. Such formulas lingered deep within the arithmetic so dear to a gambler's soul.

Seeing Jim poke through the door, George jumped down awkwardly from one of the high seats. "Sir, welcome. Privilege to see you this fine morning, Boss." Jim clambered up into the chair and planted his shoes, ready for polishing, on the two brass footrests.

He opened one of the papers. Over the top of it he watched the crown of George's ancient bald head. The man's body was hobbled by circumstance and time, but the long brown hands were still nimble, applying polish the way an artist brushes on paint, daubing it with his fingertips, never getting so much as a dust-sized speck of white on the black parts or vice versa, running the shoe rag over the leather with a rhythm as regular as a steam locomotive's, a special snap and pop every now and then demonstrating his technique.

"Always a pleasure to serve you, Mr. J.," Taggart concluded. He pocketed his tip with the discretion of a first-rate maître d'. "You got a glaze on them moccasins, Mr. J."

As Jim thanked him and walked out the door, George called after him, "Mr. J, sir, have you forgot your newspapers?"

"I'll leave them for the next guy," Jim said. He had only needed to glance at the front pages. Across the top of the *State-Journal* one-star edition ran the header ANOTHER MYSTERIOUS LIQUOR SHOOTING. Below, in smaller type, FEARS 'LEGGER WAR HEATING UP. The first edition of the *Register* had the Szabo story on page three.

Jim still hadn't had any breakfast but he continued walking all the way down to the Triangle to meet Pete. When he got there, Pete had already had his coffee. Jim was served one the moment he slid his body into the booth.

"How's Szabo?"

"Still barely able to talk. The cops have got just one rookie at the hospital, guarding the room. What about the chief?"

Jim smiled weakly. "I wasn't able to talk either. Not that he knew anything to ask. The man's a fool. After the election he'll be back in real estate, closing deals on bungalows, if he isn't going door to door with Fuller brushes. Either way it's the same pitch. 'There, there, Mrs. McGillacuddy, here's the one for you.'"

"What do we do if this character doesn't croak like a frog?"

"Nothing, because he's got nothing on us. It wasn't our goods he jacked, it was somebody else's. We should give him a medal. Every customer that's not satisfied is another one for us. The guy can't squeak because he's got nothing to tell 'em. What's he going to say? 'There's competition in the liquor business.' That'll make a headline in Clouse's rag."

Pete looked shocked and solemn. "You mean you don't get it? Remember that guy who got pinned in the Eighth Street Shuffle?"

"What about him?"

"He was on a job for Szabo. Doing jobs for that bunch whenever he could. This time you were the job. I know, because I walked him back all the way to a fellow in Youngstown who was the go-between's go-between."

Jim sat silent for a moment. "You sure about this?"

Sells nodded up and down. "Positive."

"Jesus, Pete. This stuff's gotta stop. Right now. Else we'll never win our election."

Jim didn't say any more but merely shook his head and looked into his coffee cup as though it were possible to read the dregs the way some old woman might read tea leaves.

Cynthia McConnell:

Mummy and Daddy believed strongly that my brother and I should perform unpaid and useful work during school breaks and such, rather than merely playing tennis with our friends and things such as that. So it was that I was one of the volunteer girls doing noble chores at Passavant Hospital. This included making regular half-hour checks on seriously ill or injured patients, cheering them up, supposedly, when the nurses were busy with more important duties. When I looked in on one Mr. Harold Szabo I thought at first that he was unconscious. But no—he certainly wasn't moving much, except his piteously weak vocal chords, which had been damaged but not severed in the apparent accident that had brought him there. He could still speak, if somewhat less audibly than before and only with the utmost effort. I had to lean in so closely that I could smell his sickness, as I imagine he could smell my own youthfulness and the scent of my soap. "Sunny Beach," he said. "Sunny Beach." He whispered the words a third time.

"What place is that, Mr. Szabo?'

He gurgled. I continued, softly. "Is that were you're from? Sounds lovely. Is that in Florida?"

"Goddamned Sunny Beach," he said. Then all at once his throat seemed to seize up and he fell back onto the pillow.

I shrieked for help. The young policeman, who was flirting with a nurse two rooms down, sprang into action with giant steps, followed by a doctor not far behind. Officer Nolte, for that was his name, shooed everyone out of the room and began taking notes.

I had never seen a person actually expire; the only dead body I had ever seen was Grandmother McConnell's in her expensive coffin. I wasn't the same afterward and wouldn't resume being so for a long time. I told Father that I was reduced to sobs and tears by what I had seen. I begged to be excused from volunteer works until I recovered. Father agreed. Yet I noted a few years later that I had barely alluded to the incident in my diary, which was largely about being bored and going to the movies and, most of all, about boys.

Edwin Staffel:

Candidates wishing to fill Szabo's shoes were lining up like horse-players at the two-dollar window. Men—who hardly any members of the public had ever heard of yesterday—were suddenly famous when the morning papers came out with the details of their murders.

A man named Shemanski, in his mid-thirties, had been nonchalantly exiting a pool room shortly before eleven p.m. when two men stepped out of the darkness into the light of the street lamps for a few seconds. They shot him four times, then slithered back into the night. They had arrogantly selected a moment when the eleven-to-seven shift was coming on at McConnell Steel, ensuring maximum hubbub and a big crowd of gawkers. The coroner, the gin blossoms on his face glimmering under the street lamp, later told the press that a passbook from a Detroit bank had been found in the man's clothing showing a balance of over nine thousand. The coroner, Haberkamp, had a nose like a champagne cork and a voice like a busted calliope.

"Was he heavy when he got baked?" the pesky reporter from the *State Journal* wished to know.

"What's that, young man?"

"Was he carrying a weapon?"

"You'd have to ask the police that one."

As he usually did, Haberkamp then carefully spelled his own name for the assembled newspapermen.

Within weeks, a mildly prominent hoodlum, a local this time, was also sheared: three bullets from a .32-20. There were lots of small guns in those days. Pocket guns, almost. Hold-out pieces. Not like before, or later. The police announced that they could not rule out the possibility of foul play. Justice was swiftly attempted. The *Enterprise* followed the lack of developments closely. The topic eventually ended up in a one-column story deep inside the paper, "Murder Cause Still Mystery After Inquest: Callas Witnesses Seem Reluctant." "Bound by a code which does not tolerate 'squealers,'" the story began, "eight witnesses placed on the stand in a coroner's inquest last night refused to shed any light upon the motive which led to the slaying of local gambling figure Theodore Callas, 27, who was shot to death at the Esquire Lunch Room."

Those who were there remembered it as sickening. The Greek gentleman in question fell face down into his seventy-five-cent special, well after the soup but in the middle of the roast pork loin with jardinière potatoes.

Before the police finally filed the case under Pending For Review, there were three or four more shootings, one of them on the steps of the Pythian Castle. The *State Journal* took special delight in running a photograph of the blood-stained victim lying arms akimbo in an undignified contortion next to his upside-down hat. The picture ran on the front page next to a rare page-one editorial written by Clouse himself, comparing the city uncomplimentarily to both Sodom and Gomorrah. Clouse's conclusion was to endorse the soon-to-be-official mayoral candidacy of William Haberkamp, the fearless and long-serving coroner, an incorruptible civic leader who knew better than anyone else—at first hand and at close range—the terror taking place in our gangster-ridden streets and who would work tirelessly to end the twin curses of bootlegging and gambling. In truth, shootings were popular with the public, much more so than dynamiting, though the latter had become almost monthly occurrences because dynamite, though often of unpredictable quality, could easily go missing from building sites and highway projects, and always expressed itself emphatically even when it was not fatal.

From the diary of Cynthia McConnell:

I'm crazy about him, that's all there is to it. I think about him and his wavy hair all the time and it gives me the shivers. I'm not as sophisticated as everyone thinks I ought to be—"with all your advantages," others keep saying to me. I know just where I am and what it is I want to be. I'm not just another silly pill like so many of the other girls.

Of the fellows I've ever kissed, Duncan is the one I most enjoy it with. I think he must be some kind of artist in kissing. He tells me that not many girls are good kissers. "You wouldn't think that, with all the practice most of them get." What a cheeky boy! Once I told Hedy—she's the only person in this house I'm really able to talk to—that before Duncan I didn't care to be kissed so much because everyone always seems to draw my life into theirs and I hate that. Hedy said that the way I felt was partly my fault, because it takes two and if I don't contribute more than my fair share then I've only myself to blame. Hedy is the wisest person I know.

Allan Ostermeyer:

The men came, one at a time at intervals, to a small suite in the Hotel Florence, for they would be too conspicuous at the Congress.

"About this election," Jim began. "I suppose we should begin with what we all know: Haberkamp is too stupid even to be the coroner, much less the mayor. He doesn't even have a medical degree."

"But before that he was an alderman in the old Fifth Ward," someone chimed in, "for I can't remember how many terms."

"True enough," Jim said, "but memories get short when those who used to find jobs for the boys suddenly snap up the good ones themselves."

A third voice piped up. "We all know what's going to

happen here. Metzger and his lapdog Clouse are running Haberkamp on an anti-crime platform, shutting down what's local and bringing in the dry agents to smash up the speaks. The *State Journal*, that rag"—he made a gesture imitating spitting—"is just waiting for its chance for a caper like this."

"All that's true," Jim said, "except the part about places being shut down permanently. But listen to my plan. We pick a sitting alderman that people seem to like."

Pete, sitting in the corner, was rolling a toothpick from one side of his mouth to the other. "A Lebanese, like Mike Jalad maybe?"

"No, Mike's too honest. Honest to a fault. Besides the guy we run against Haberkamp can't be Lebanese. This is something I learned up in Montreal. At first glance, the greaseballs, the Greeks, and the Irish run everything, but they can't stay in power without sharing with other people. Some Jews are very big up there, even some Chinese, all sorts of guys. There's this French fellow, living in the middle of this half-English city, keeping it all in balance, so people from one old country aren't always going to war with people from some other old country. It needs to be the same here maybe. Or it could be."

"Now, I've spoken with Henry Klein. We've had long talks. His public advantages are his good name in city politics—alderman, helped get schools and streetcar shelters built, nice guy, has less enemies than anybody else who's been in the public eye that long—almost none, not serious ones, not ones we know about. And his other strong point: he's never made a habit of mentioning to anyone that he supports a wide-open form of government. Believe me, I know that he does. I know it so well that I'm prepared to put myself on the line to be the scapegoat."

By now, some of the others in the room were leaning far forward in their seats.

"I propose we run Klein as an even more ferocious crime buster than Haberkamp. Fiery speeches that would make Clouse's editorials look sissified. All the while, the *Register* would be digging into Haberkamp's last seven or eight years and finding that he's consistently ruined evidence. Hell, the press might even discover that he's been robbing the stiffs in the morgue."

Jim looked over at McConnell. "These would be good stories, would they not?" McConnell answered with a lukewarm nod of well-disguised admiration. There was nothing quite like a straight-arrow with a thug's heart. Jim continued. "There's the union angle as well." He glanced at McConnell. "All those men you have at the mills."

He didn't need to point out that virtually all of them, the foreign-borns especially, were habitual non-Republicans to begin with. "They need to be better informed about Clouse's anti-union slant on the world. We can cover every house in those parts of town with somebody that speaks whatever language the guy who opens the front door spoke as a kid, or still does. Clouse's ravings about restricting immigration could stand some rehashing."

Jim finally dropped the big one. "This is going to be a tough race. But at just the right moment we'll have my places raided by the dry agents. I'll be arrested. Picture it: me in cuffs being led away, Klein holding onto my arm like he's the arresting officer, the photographers, all of them, from all the papers, flashing away left and right. The king of the underworld"—he laughed sarcastically—"finally put away and the streets made safe. Klein will look like the greatest rackets buster since—I don't know who. Of course I won't come up for a hearing until after the election."

The obvious question popped up. "What happens if you can't beat the rap. I mean, this would be federal stuff, am I right?"

Jim was the picture of clever optimism. "All we have to do to beat the rap is to win the election. Then we'll have peace all round. I am a man of peace."

Pete, in a corner at the back of the room, snorted to himself.

Cynthia McConnell:

"My little girl is going to be eighteen!"

"Yes, Father, I know."

"So your mother and I thought we should have a talk about the future." His tone was appropriately parental.

I always experienced a dry taste of apprehension when I was in his study. Even though I was intrigued by his display of old guns, for example, I tried never to let it show. This was a room for business, his business.

"When I was a young fellow, I had my year in Europe, just as your mother had hers. And your brother. Experiences that last a lifetime, as you've heard me say so often before. Your mother and I feel you should have the same opportunities. You've told us of your ambition to design dresses. It's not a subject I profess to know much about, but where could there be a better place than Paris to learn about such things?"

"No, I want to stay here and design a new kind of clothes for ordinary American women."

"Ordinary. That doesn't sound like there's much ambition involved."

"Well, that's what I want to do. I'm very serious about it."

He paused a moment. "So, then, you have been offered your year abroad but have chosen to spend it at home. I suppose that's all right. But what about college? You've said that you don't wish to go to your mother's old school. She found that statement difficult to accept at first, but I believe I've brought her round. A new generation, new teaching methods I suppose, new ideas for new times, all of that. So we've been thinking of Hollins. We hope you'll apply. This is our wish, your mother's and mine."

Poor Father, I thought. Here he was trying to be reasonable and conciliatory, as though my life were some big business arrangement and he was enjoying a drink at the Pantheon Club, feeling about for some common ground. I knew how that worked, so I didn't make a fuss just yet.

It seemed the meeting would be mercifully brief this

time, but that hope soon evaporated.

"There's one more topic on the agenda. I hear from your mother and from Earle Hamilton at the club that his son Duncan and you have been seeing each other socially. I suppose this is really a conversation that your mother should be having with you." (I was saying to myself: God no, spare me that, O Lord.) "I've known the Hamiltons for years. They've been in banking in this city for longer than most people can recollect. When I was an adolescent I actually heard elderly people refer to 'Hamilton's Bank,' as though that were its name. Earle tells me that Duncan is being brought right along in the business. I'm told his talent lies in the area of trusts—managing people's estates for the benefit of the surviving family members. Not the most exciting part of banking, I grant you, but a good service to society and a market that's there to be met.

"The point I'm coming to is that he seems to be a fine hard-working young man with an assured future. But remember that he is older than you by a number of years. Again, this is a part of our talk that your mother could handle with more grace and far less embarrassment. But I'll say it the best way I know how. If you fall in love with him, be sure he's the right man for you." He obviously had been debating with himself about what he should say in conclusion. "And even if you don't, be careful."

"Yes, Father. Thank you."

I left the room, permitting him, I'm sure, to lean back in his padded chair and say to himself, *Damned if that didn't go far better than I'd expected. McConnell, you've still got it in you.*

Edwin Staffel:

Pete had never set foot across the border, first because he didn't have to, second because he was heartily sick to death of hearing Jim talk on and on about the grandeur of Montreal with its sophistication, its malleable authorities and, what he found most irksome of all, its Negro jazz clubs. Sometimes Jim would talk out loud about opening a place like that here. "Nobody'd go for it," Pete would say. "People aren't so open-minded down here." Anyway, he thought, things were tough enough already.

To some extent, that was true. Clouse had been getting everyone worked up. One day the *State-Journal* actually ran an editorial about "The Dark Side of the Night Clubs." The piece denounced the Paddock and the Allies as pernicious influences on the life of the city as a whole and in particular its young women, many of whom were being turned into flappers, morally adrift in a sea of sin, and its honest workingmen, who were now exposed not only to indigenous criminals but to even worse ones from out of town. People would be lured to the Triangle where their hearts beat in time to the flashing lights. There was no reference to race as such; there didn't have to be. Obviously someone had been telling Clouse about Jim's daydream.

"I don't mean to say there's a lynch mob..." Pete said.

"I'm sure Clouse won't mind if there was."

"I'm just saying that some are afraid there might be trouble."

"Well, Clouse has enough trouble of his own at the

moment. Which might give us an opportunity. We'll see. I'm going to check into it a little bit today and try to work some diplomacy. Anyway, the point is we've got to get more with the times. That's the lesson I've been getting from the big man in Montreal. He is a very smart fellow. You'll see for yourself when he finally comes for a visit. I don't know when that will be. Hell, he even stays away from places where somebody might take his picture. But sometime. Sooner, not later."

Pete was left to utter inanities. "Well, they got a whole different country up there. What works in one place won't necessarily work someplace else."

"True. But you've got to keep yourself open to good ideas when you see them. You ought to come up there with me one of these times. I know, I keep saying that."

"But who'd look after the store?" Sells asked. "I got my hands full."

Jim kept his mouth shut.

Cynthia McConnell:

One day I waited until Hedy stepped out into the garden to pick parsley for the dish she was preparing for dinner.

"How are you today, child?" White children seemed to like being addressed that way, but Hedy, for the sake of dignity and the never-ending search for a bit of precious respect, used the word as a joke, a sort of nickname, and only with me, never with my brother.

"Well, I've got a question for you," I said. "It's really, really embarrassing to talk about." Who else could I possibly go to for help? Not Mummy. Never. My mother spent the greater portion of each year in bed, sleeping it off or being lonely and depressed. The rest of the time she spent in Paris.

"Is this what you call a problem with a woman's plumbing?" Hedy lowered her voice, though there was no one remotely close enough to overhear us. "You aren't expecting a package from Railway Express, are you?"

I shook my head no and relief brushed across Hedy's expressive old face. I cleared my throat.

"Questions get asked without us having to do any of the work, but they don't answer themselves. Tell me what's troubling your mind."

"You know I've been going out with Duncan Hamilton for quite a while now."

Hedy nodded. She had helped raise him during her time at the Hamilton place.

"We, well, go to bed together quite a bit."

"Go on."

I lowered my voice, to a whisper. "You see, it's great at the time, but—how should I put this—he's so big, down there, that it hurts afterward, hurts really bad."

There was a pause.

"What you say is no surprise to me," Hedy finally said. "His daddy is the same way. So was his granddaddy."

I looked at her for a moment, before we both collapsed in laughter.

Hedy prescribed Arm & Hammer baking soda in the bath water, her remedy for many of life's ailments.

Allan Ostermeyer:

Henry Klein was a decent man who looked like someone who had spent his whole life trying unsuccessfully to attract the waiter's attention. He was also someone who needed money. He didn't have a pension or much in the way of savings to help get his kids started, or money to leave to his wife when he went. He had hardly ever been more than fifty miles from where he was born, but that's the way he wished to live. He wasn't just a do-gooder but a patriot as well—to his wife and family, to his ward, to his hometown, and to the Democratic Party. He had surrendered to the blandishments of Jim Joseph and the others, but once the mud began to fly he started to doubt his wisdom in agreeing to have anything to do with the mayoral election of 1928.

The fight got underway when the *Register* began pointing out that Haberkamp had no medical training and had been withholding knowledge that the police and the courts needed to carry out their functions. Moreover— this was emphasized—victims' families were deprived the comfort they deserved during their bereavement. In a sense, the paper suggested, Haberkamp's lack of a medical education of any type, including an understanding of simple Boy Scout first aid, was tantamount to defrauding the public. McConnell's editor-in-chief then commenced a campaign to require a specialized degree from a reputable educational institution for anyone aspiring to be a coroner anywhere in the state. For its part, the *State Journal* made a display of Haberkamp's service in the Great War while charging Klein with being a draft dodger, though, born in 1885, Klein, at thirty-two, had probably been too old to be a common soldier for the draft in 1917, though men his age still had to get draft cards.

Register subscribers, or those few equipped to read so deeply between the lines, were permitted to infer that Haberkamp was involved in some sort of hanky-panky with the corpses in his custody—whether something as simple as accepting tips in exchange for nudging distraught relatives to certain undertakers or something unspeakably ghastly, no one could say for certain. In the next edition, Klein promised that if elected he would order a prompt and thorough investigation, while the rival paper suggested that he must first investigate himself and the corruption rife in his entire campaign. The front page of the *Register* screeched outrage. Those who read the piece and the accompanying editorial to the end were assured that Haberkamp was the hand-puppet of the bootleggers, murderers and thieves who were funding his campaign and ruining the city's fully deserved reputation as a Christian paradise held hostage by gangsters of foreign birth. As for their part in this free exchange of opinion, the *State Journal*'s team of reporters proved, daily, even twice a day, that Klein was an elderly political hanger-on of the lowest order, the blind and spavined stalking horse of the notorious bootlegger and gambler who called himself James Joseph. Each candidate claimed to be more anti-crime than the others.

The harshest blow was dealt by Clouse's men who by matching dusty tax records with old files about prostitution arrests were able to show that in previous times a row of small wooden houses had once been (and could still be? or once again might become?) houses of ill fame owned by McConnell Steel. These charges blew the city sky high.

At a public meeting, McConnell asserted that these identical, modest dwellings had been built as perquisites to help lure skilled workers from various places in eastern Europe. "As I understand it, my friends, this was the common practice in the iron and steel industry long before the turn of the century, back when my Grandfather McConnell was still at the helm. What else these dwellings might have been used for, I cannot say. I assure you that they were not bordellos. At one time, one of them may have served as meeting rooms for the Sons of Poland or some similar group." His words were few, but they managed to turn the churches and some of the unionized foreigners against what Clouse's paper now delighted to call, in headlines, editorials and even cartoons, "Redlight Democrats."

When Joseph and McConnell next met, the former quickly whispered to the latter, "I shut the houses down that instant. Tight as a drum. Don't worry." But McConnell was furious at this assault on his reputation and on his home life. Mrs. McConnell had told him to go to hell; he told her to go back to Paris for a while, which she did, none too steadily and with her wrath not lessened one bit. His son was taking it straight up but Cynthia was acting like someone on the verge of a nervous collapse.

Thankfully Mrs. McConnell was already on the liner when Clouse printed an interview with an elderly gentleman, a sporting man in his distant youth whom the passage of time had rendered charming, in a risqué kind of way that some ladies at the Altenheim pretended, for his benefit, to be shocked by. As the old man spun folktales about the early days, two *State Journal* reporters made notes.

"My father and me would go into the Triangle every week to sell what we had for cash money. When I was sixteen, he told me it was time to learn about life, to prepare myself, you see. He took me to one of these houses and spoke some quiet words with this Negro woman who was in charge. I can see her yet. She was a beauty and wore a red gown—I'd never seen anything like it before. She called herself, or else others called her, Lady Henrietta. Lady Something anyway; I don't remember exactly. What I remember is she was what the young people would call a firecracker."

The reporters pressed for more details, any scraps of recollection. The old fellow was finding it difficult. "The only other thing I can tell you is that long after this, maybe, I don't know, thirty years later, some friend of mine, his name's gone out of head just now, told me that she eventually retired, you might say, and is working in one of the big houses. Anyway, just gossip. She must be long dead, I suppose." One reporter excused himself and went back to the paper. In the middle of the newsroom he saw the publisher shouting, as usual. "Excuse me, Mr. Clouse. I think we've got a nice piece of steak for you." It turned out to be two days' worth of nameless innuendo, though they still got it in the paper. Speaking professionally, I kept hoping that a writ of libel would follow, but none did.

Edwin Staffel:

Two weeks to go and no one could foresee the outcome. At first, every bookmaker you talked to gave you slightly different odds, but only slightly. The needle refused to move. Finally they had no choice but to consider the race as even money on a dead heat.

The Joseph-Sells combination put in long hours organizing, with special emphasis on certain parts of the population. Speakers of every language ever heard anywhere on the streets, running a broken alphabet from Armenian to Welsh, were addressed in their native tongues. Crowds gathered in every ward. Intermediaries paid by Pete ensured especially good turnouts at the American Legion post, the union halls, the local clubs, and the full range of fraternal lodges.

There were slip-ups, inevitably. A featured speaker failed to materialize (he'd suffered an honest accident, as it happened) and Pete had to take the podium. The audience wanted to hear discussion of the crime issue. Pete, however, was dressed in such a flashy manner, with two bodyguards standing at either end of the stage, with their hands in their pockets, and still wearing their hats, that the citizens in attendance were forced to conclude that they were seeing the crime issue in the flesh. Besides, Pete was a terrible speaker. He had a jailhouse accent, though it was actually the result of the war.

A meeting, mercifully one without Pete, was held in what the Negro Knights of Pythias called its auditorium, which doubled as a movie hall when all-Negro motion pictures could be found. A self-ordained clergyman from what he called his tabernacle spoke about what the outcome of this election would mean for non-whites. Toward the end he was interrupted by an angry man who bitterly demanded to know why Caucasians were being paid eight or ten dollars for their votes while their own kind were lucky to get four or five.

The reverend was as quick on his feet as he was eloquent. "As all of you here this evening know, the railroad depot has two waiting rooms, one for whites, the other for us. Some of you more elderly folks may say the proof of progress is the fact that the two are exactly the same, same size, same everything, from top to bottom. If your starting point is somewhere way back in history, you might say there was a time when we weren't allowed on the trains at all—not as passengers. Later they gave us our own cars and a separate seating for meals. Eventually the situation improved. We purchase our tickets for the price the white travellers pay. Progress has been slow, but we must never let it stop altogether. Equality in all departments of life is our goal." There was a ragged chorus of mumbles and shouts from some. "And equality will be arrived at over time and only through the pursuit of dignity, struggled for in a dignified way."

Someone at the back of the hall rose for a rebuttal, saying that he would withhold his vote until he was paid the same as a white man. A number of others nodded or murmured in agreement. "Else," the man said, "I won't vote at all and both parties will suffer a little."

In the final week before what some with longer memories were calling the most dramatic and hotly contested local election since that of 1888, virtually identical news stories dominated the front pages.

The *Register* and the *State Journal* told the story with halftones right below their nameplates and running almost to the fold, the copy jumping from the front to two inside pages. Both were printed on the Goss Comet Perfecting Press, a fast rotary job that even folded the papers, a function that caused grumbling among the small battalion of men and women who had done the work by hand. As for the *Inter-Ocean*, its photographic reproduction was poor and mottled, and the whole printing process harmfully retrograde. It was still using its old flatbed press, the Duplex Model A, which performed only with sufficient coaxing, cursing, and praying.

The *Enterprise* was somewhere in the middle. On that day they showed pictures of Jim Joseph, wearing a flat cap rather than a hat with a brim. Handcuffed by one of the two dry agents, Joseph was taken in hand by William

Klein, who was trying his best to look fierce as the prisoner stepped into the back of the patrol wagon. The *Register*'s head, JAMES 'JIM' JOSEPH ARRESTED BY KLEIN AT TRI-ANGLE NIGHT SPOT, extended across all eight columns. A subhead bellowed, "Mayoral Front-Runner William ('Rackets-Buster') Klein Vows to End Crime in City."

All the papers and radio broadcasting stations recounted how a large squad of federal Prohibition agents and state law officers used axes and sledgehammers to break down the door of the Paddock Club, but were unable to do so before most of the liquor, which claimed to be bonded, had been disposed of. The agents used sponges and even eye-droppers to gather enough evidence to show that the place was indeed the site of illegal activity. Then they destroyed the twenty-foot bar, the interior doors, and the lattice work meant to indicate that the establishment was a cozy family-run affair. Various customers and staff escaped, one by jumping out a second-storey window, twisting or possibly snapping an ankle. But Jim was nabbed. His fearful expression turned into a smile once the door of the paddy wagon closed behind him, headed for temporary storage at the municipal jail at City Hall. Until his arraignment he would be held on a thousand-dollar bond—to Jim, a penny ante bet. His lawyer managed to get the court date postponed until the day after the election. The dark low-ceilinged cells were nine feet long and five across, equipped only with a chamber pot and a wooden bed, smaller than a bench at the streetcar Waiting Room and without even a blanket. Jim stretched out and relaxed.

Once the polls closed at seven p.m., the ballot boxes were brought one at a time, under police guard, to the city council room. There, volunteers counted the ballots under the close supervision of bipartisan invigilators. At forty-three minutes to midnight it was announced that Klein had defeated Haberkamp by a little more than four thousand votes.

A few moments later Pete Sells, dressed for a night on the town, carried out one of his original ideas, the kind that Jim tolerated. He entered the council chamber with a few of his pug-uglies standing respectfully behind him, and distributed expensive solid-silver cigarette cases, ones he considered quite high-tone, engraved with the day, month, and year. Like malevolent Santas, the thugs helped to hand them around. The electoral officials, cops, and volunteers seemed startled.

Cynthia McConnell wasn't old enough to cast a vote. But as her father didn't wish to be seen publicly in connection with the mayor's race, he had asked her to hang about at City Hall and call him from one of the telephone booths in the lobby as soon as the outcome was official. She was still down there, waiting for Duncan to come by and pick her up in his flivver when Pete and his entourage came clattering smoothly down the staircase. She caught his eye, and he gave her a leftover cigarette case. "Here you go, doll-face, a souvenir for you." He and his friends disappeared into the night, but the swing of victory in the man's step stayed with Cynthia for many nights.

From the diary of Cynthia McConnell:

Since the election I've hardly even spoken to Hedy. There was a rumour about her younger days that the newspapers tried to make into an issue, but they couldn't use her name, thanks to Father, I believe, and the fact that all those who have known what the truth was and what it wasn't had dried up or died off. Vicious gossip, that's all it was. It would embarrass her if she even thought I had understood what the fuss was about. She would lose face, which makes me very sad, because I still somehow feel that something has broken between us. She was always the only person I could talk with about absolutely anything, but we'll sure never be able to talk about this.

I've been designing a new outfit. I've made sketch after sketch; I'm quite good at coming up with fashion ideas, I think. I always have a bunch of them. I asked Hedy to help me cut out the paper pattern which I then took to a good seamstress. It's awfully cute and looks great on me. It's a black skirt of silk crepe with two double pleats in the front and back. It comes up high in front and back and has very narrow shoulder straps. It fits me so snugly and has a belt about two inches wide with a round silver buckle. I found earrings to match the buckle. I need to look my best for a special occasion. This is what I'll be wearing when I break up with Duncan... I've been outgrowing him, I think, in the same way I'm outgrowing this diary now that I'm becoming more serious.

Allan Ostermeyer:

As everybody found out once Cynthia McConnell's diary was introduced as evidence in the trial—and some of the juicy bits were printed in all the papers except the *Register*—she was trying to figure out what a woman who might go out with Pete Sells should look like and how she should act. As a result, she was shortening all her skirts and dresses. While she was at it, she pursued a much more detailed interest in cosmetics. She also did something her father had always demanded she not do: she had her hair cut into a Dutch bob. Hedy would help her sneak out the back way on certain evenings when she was supposed to be performing good works. Which is precisely what she was doing down in the Triangle: being a volunteer in the life of a dynamo who brilliantined his hair, didn't keep regular hours, had thousands in his pockets, and—as she learned one night when they were dancing particularly close—kept a fat-ass revolver in his waistband. Cynthia also began asking everyone never again to call her by her Christian name. From now on, she would be Thidi, with an i. She remembered reading in some magazine or other that this was the name of a famous Queen of Burma. Oriental.

Edwin Staffel:

It wasn't easy—the defendant had to keep from grinning, and the authorities swallowed hard—but eventually the government vacated their case against Jim. To celebrate, he decided to go back to Montreal. In the time since his last visit, the Carpenter had become far heavier. He really stood out in any group of other French-Canadian men, so much so that you had to wonder whether he had a condition or just a freakish appetite. He was a soft-spoken man, but his physical presence was starting to make him look threatening. In New York or Chicago, say, this would have been a healthy advantage in the liquor and gambling trades. Up there it made him a memorable and instantly recognizable figure, at least in certain circles, I mean. Among, for example, people who used one name during the day and another one at night.

From what he knew already about the city and himself, Jim felt that Montreal was his other city, endlessly fascinating, where just about anything, if it didn't happen on its own accord, might be made to happen somehow.

In a quiet corner of a loud café, Jim and the Carpenter were chatting about business.

"This, ah, interdiction from below down there, this Prohibition, it is not going to last forever." So said the Carpenter.

"Everybody knows that except my partner," Jim replied. "I think the years of easy money, big money, have changed his thinking, you know."

"Changed how?"

"Made him into a different person than he was before. He has a big swagger—you know 'swagger'?"

"Yes, I think so."

"He lives alone—permanently, I think—in one entire floor of a fancy little apartment hotel. As a gambler he's reckless, no sense whatever. When he loses, he throws money around as though he just won big-time. Hundred-dollar tips for waiters, even for doormen, because he wants to be recognized and remembered, and that's not always a good way for someone in our trade to be. He keeps eleven automobiles in a garage downtown. He has thirty or forty hand-stitched suits in his closet. One time a cleaner's delivery boy returning a couple of them on hangers handed him a note from the owner of the shop. It said: 'These were found in front trouser pocket of the dark worsted. I know you would want them returned.' With the note were two thousand-dollar bills. Now, few in town have ever handled even one banknote like that; everybody else probably has never actually *seen* one. Two thousand bucks in any form is more than some poor working stiff might take home in a year."

The Carpenter chuckled deeply, from inside out, as only a large man can do.

"I notice you say 'town.' I have often wondered this: Why do Americans call their cities towns? This seems strange to me. A place is a city, or a small town, or a village, but the words don't have the same meaning."

"Nobody's ever asked me this before. I don't really

know how to answer except to say that when we call a city a town it's a way of showing our affection for it. It's when we have a fine automobile that works perfectly and we call it a wreck or a heap."

The Carpenter knew "wreck" as something that is no longer working at all because it has fallen apart. A total loss, like a ship that's been wrecked. "Heap to me is a big pile of something. Like coal you buy all at once to heat your house in winter."

"Or junk. 'A heap of junk.'"

"I would bet that your partner doesn't talk about his eleven automobiles in this way."

"If he did, it would only be to sound tougher. He's a tough guy."

The Carpenter was curious about this character, and Jim wasn't hesitant to give him the lowdown. "He's my wife's older brother. We bought a little taxi business together. That's all it was until a fellow hired us to pick up a load of booze from a warehouse of yours. That's how we started making enough to expand, to get into the business ourselves."

"The man who hired you to drive for him. Who was he?"

"I'd never heard of him before." Jim thought it best to prevent follow-up questions. "Later he was murdered."

The Carpenter wrinkled his broad, high and fleshy forehead and held his palms out to the sides. "Too bad."

"Personally, I don't care for the violence," Jim said.

"I am of that same belief. So many people die so that

the others, the grand fishes, the ones who still swim in the water, can take even more. The problem has been much more terrible in places like New York or Detroit, or in some smaller places like your Kansas City. That's partly because they're still fighting about what they can buy from us up here. But it happens in Montreal as well."

Jim loved the way the Montrealers pronounced their city's name.

The Carpenter went on: "On the map of the world, we are only—what is the term? I know but I cannot remember it now." Later, alone in bed, the phrase finally came to him: accessories. "This whole business, it is not a moral way to live." He looked sad—heavy and sad. "But that has never stopped us, has it?"

As the evening grew longer, conversation circled back to the question about what life would be like after Prohibition.

"Oh, there will always be ways of making money, including some old ways. These changes happen all the time. Not money like the money in the past ten years, of course, but there will always be ways if we're smart. The trick is to save and invest, not just spend, the way your friend does. We have to keep the stuff coming through the front door without spending as much money as we used to do."

Jim got a sense that the Carpenter was referring to the two of them, maybe working together, rather than to what the *State Journal* described as frequently as possible as the "criminal element." He saw that his friend may have had this feeling for a couple of years already.

"Congress in Washington has pushed through the Jones Act," Jim said.

"I have read about this."

"It means tougher sentences for leggers and more trouble with the federal people all the way around. But everybody knows it's also probably the last thing to happen before Prohibition finally gets cancelled." He paused. "You must have quite a bit of money stashed outside Canada."

"That's the most personal question you can ask a man." The big gentleman looked stern for a moment. After a careful but effective silence, his face, just beginning to fall into dewlaps, took on a smile. The Carpenter was an excellent actor. Perhaps that was one of his weapons, or at least one of his deal-making techniques. "I don't know why I like your company," he said. "But I do. We're becoming friends quick, eh? Friends. Am I right?"

"In English, you'd probably say fast friends. But, yes, we are, I agree."

Each man tipped the lip of his highball glass in the other's direction.

"Then can I ask you questions, between friends, about your present situation down there?"

"Well, we were successful because I'm a good organizer. This became more important once we stopped relying on importing stuff from Montreal for the finished product." To once again indicate his loyalty, he spread his arms wide in a gesture of admiration for the place and its people. "There were other small-timers, but they stopped operating when my brother-in-law convinced them. I didn't like this way of working, but nobody wanted to be our partners. They feared him. They were happier working alone."

The Carpenter was quite attentive.

"Our product was good but we didn't have the kind of variety the joint-owners, or their customers, wanted. So we added a fine selection of what we made on the spot. Out-of-state groups paid very big money for the distilleries, and breweries too, that were padlocked in 1920, but most of the still work done in these places was sent to bigger cities. They only took away a little of our business, that's all. I leased an empty warehouse, an innocent-looking place from the outside, and began making stuff for export as well as for the local stiffs. We made bad beer as well as whatever spirits a person might want: genuine, imported or domestic, and a whole menu of possibilities involving tinted water and grain alcohol. There aren't many Lebanese down there. We're not like the Greeks. But I must have had every Lebanese household in town mixing stuff.

"Our prices were fair by the standards back then, and our deliveries were on time. The amount of discretion, it went up and down, according to the pressure on us. Anyway, the point is that I used my gambler's head and a bit of luck to make the system run right."

"And the authorities you paid?"

"It's funny, the squeeze didn't come from the dry agents, who were mostly dirty, or from the competition, at least not after some of my partner's methods became rougher than they liked and everybody settled down a bit.

The problem was the local cops, the preachers and priests, jealous businessmen in some other trade, a judge or two, and all but one of the papers. To operate safely, I needed to elect a new mayor who would do what we tell him. Such as appointing a police chief who's greedy and keeps quiet. Well, we did it, let us say only that. It had to be done. But it's going to end up with me paying out a lot more soup."

"Soup?"

Joseph put down his glass for a second and rubbed his right thumb with two fingers.

"*La soupe*, that's a good one. Here we say *pot-de-vin*— much bigger! It needs a *soupière* that is giant-size. Like my belly!" The man's sudden self-deprecation surprised Jim, who went back to work on his cocktail.

"You have invested for when it rains?" the Carpenter asked.

"Real estate," Jim replied. "I own the apartment building I live in and an office building or two, and of course the two buildings my cafés are in. They're real dumps, down in the old part of town where I grew up. My lawyer has set up each one as a private company. Associates of mine hold most of the shares, but when they receive dividend checks I go to them and have a talk."

"You split with your partner?"

"Yes." But the word had an uncertain ring to it.

From the diary of Cynthia McConnell:

Sitting on the edge of the bathtub I could see him in the mirror standing there looking back at me. The pyjama top I was wearing didn't fall much below my hips, and when I bent over to reach for a cigarette he got a good view down the front. I didn't mind, I just hoped he wouldn't cut himself. He carefully unfolded the razor and ran the steel edge back and forth across the strop hanging by the basin. Next to the tin of tooth powder was a cake of shaving soap in a mug. He stirred up some white frothy lather and applied it to both sides of his face as though he were painting a fence. He pulled his jowls taunt to make a flat surface for the blade. The scraping sound was soft and chilling, suggesting both beauty and violence. With his left hand he held his nostrils up out of harm's way while he did the space where his moustache used to be when he had one (I'd asked him to get rid of it please). I was surprised at how slowly he worked yet how efficient he seemed and how confident. When he was done, he inspected the job, washed away leftover bits of foam and patted himself dry with a fresh hand towel. I had never seen my father shave, or my brother either. The McConnell family is private even about unimportant things. I wondered whether this was an art that men taught their adolescent sons. How old would they be? Did everyone follow the same procedures in the same order? Pete splashed cologne on his newly undressed face and turned around to look at me. He was wearing the other half of the striped pyjamas. 'Sweetheart,' he said, 'you're a real blue-ribbon roadster. I have to give you that!' That night he suddenly said that my eyes were the same blue as billiard chalk.

Edwin Staffel:

A Prohibition agent called Ackerman was brought in from out of state so no one would know him or his real purpose in the city. In fact, though, his unfamiliar face aroused suspicion, not to mention the fact that he looked exactly the way a Prohibition agent would look: brown hat, brown suit, brown shoes, all cheap, probably all from the same store. Suspicion turned to hostility. Hostility wasn't hard to bring about when Sells got involved. Talk about oil and water. As Ackerman later testified, he was thirty-six, with four children, and had been a dry agent for a little more than three years, since the fall of 1925. A much younger operative, Postlewaite, who looked like a college boy, was working with him. They went to the Paddock Club in the Triangle at five p.m. on the day in question. The doorkeeper looked them over through the little sliding aperture in the door and, because Postlewaite looked so much like a college kid in search of sin, pressed the buzzer and the electric door swung open. On the ground floor, in what Ackerman called the beer bar, each of them sipped from a seidel. Then they proceeded upstairs to the whiskey bar (Ackerman's term again), consumed four shots of whiskey, and purchased a pint of some nonspecific distilled spirits to take with them. They remained in the city, at the Hotel Florence, trying to look inconspicuous and nonchalant while at the same time being nosey. Of course they failed. Even all the ordinary people who weren't being served the regular soup were all the more eager to ingratiate themselves with Jim by telling him everything that was going on: bellhops, busboys, gas jockeys, streetcar motormen, newsboys, shoe clerks, storekeepers sweeping the sidewalks outside their shops and winding their awnings up or down.

On their fifth day in town, the pair returned to the Paddock. It was three in the morning. Postlewaite told Ackerman he had never before been up that late. "You don't have children," Ackerman replied. There was a different person tending the downstairs bar this time. There was no sign of Jim Joseph, but you could hardly miss Pete. He was one of those V-shaped men, and was dressed like a highly successful mack, with a ruby stickpin in his silk necktie. What was it about him? He had presence. He had presence the way poor Postlewaite had absence.

The raid followed nine days later, at mid-evening. Patrons scrambled and scurried away but they weren't bothered or taken in. A small stock of liquor, for only a certain amount was visible at any one time, was confiscated, along with cash from the till and a small safe under one end of the bar. Only one symbolic beer keg was selected at random from among the multitude in the storage room. A roulette wheel and some other gambling equipment were hauled away in a moment of misdirected zeal, for gambling was an entirely separate matter from alcohol.

In the hearing before a federal judge, Ackerman was the sole witness for the government and gave polished testimony. He was cross-examined by the senior partner of the firm that so far had served the McConnell family

for three generations (and where the young Allan Ostermeyer had been mentored long ago). Drawing on detec-
tive work commissioned from off-duty city police under
the command of the fast-rising Sergeant Nolte, the lawyer questioned whether Ackerman and another agent (not
Postlewaite) had, on first visiting the town, met one Glad-
ys Ault and one Nora Field with the intention of taking
them across the state line for, in the legal phrase, immoral
purposes. And had he not made a date with Miss Ault and
a third young woman, Edna Mae Brechbuhler, known as
Heidi, that consisted of the three of them consuming alcohol and engaging in immoral doings? When one of the
women refused to participate in this portion of the party,
did not Agent Ackerman, flashing his badge so as to in-
timidate the jail keeper, have her placed in the municipal
jute house overnight without a commitment or warrant?
The prosecution called for a recess.

When the hearing resumed the following afternoon,
the prosecutor had no choice but to ignore what had
taken place the previous day, what with the newly freed
Heidi Brechbuhler sitting in the gallery, seething with anger at her twenty hours in one of the filthy cells atop City
Hall. The proceedings returned to the raid itself and the
actual evidence.

"Did you at any time see defendant Sells disperse alco-
holic beverages of any description?

"He was clearly in charge."

"Answer the question please. It is a yes or no question.
Which of these two words is the correct answer?"

The witness looked cross. "No, I did not, not directly."

"Speak up, please."

"No."

"Did you see the defendant either open or close the bar safe?"

"I couldn't have seen it from the other side of the whiskey bar. He was standing in front of where it was and I saw him bend down, behind the bar, but I couldn't see what he was doing there."

"So the answer is no, you did not witness him using the safe."

"Yes."

"Yes, the answer is no you did not see him do so?"

"That is correct."

Everyone knew that the hearing was only the first act of what would be an epic puppet show. Previously the forces of McConnell and Joseph on one side, Metzger and Clouse on the other, had done battle in the newspapers and, by extension, at the polls. The *State Journal* used the word "henchmen" to describe anyone who was employed by Jim, however casually or remotely. Now the United States government was involved, and some of those people were even crazier than Pete Sells, who, in a decision that shocked many, was charged, along with two barmen and a doorkeeper, with conspiring to violate the federal Prohibition laws.

Some people, I've found—analytical people—reach a certain conclusion when they find themselves in the middle of—how would you say? Some event or episode?

Some occurrence. What they do is to treat what happened the way cops are supposed to treat the scene of a violent crime. They seal it off and comb through every inch of the site for the tiniest piece of evidence. Then they think. They analyze, trying to dope out not just what took place and when and how, but even what it all suggests about what might happen later. Jim was that kind of person a bit. The Carpenter too must have been like that. Pete Sells wasn't. He'd fly into a rage immediately, throw things, break things (or people) until the situation was much worse and he was left red-faced and panting with anger. This time was certainly no different. Somebody—one of the "henchmen," I suppose—told Pete that Ackerman had left town and would presumably be back for the trial, but that Postlewaite was still around. Pete, the clean-up man and closer, caught up with Postlewaite in the Bauknecht Building downtown and knocked him down a short flight of stairs, then kicked him in the head and face until his nose and front teeth were broken. Postlewaite lay on his back, moaning inarticulately. Pete looked down at his own feet and noticed blood one of his own expensive shoes. He gripped Postlewaite's necktie to lift him off the floor and used it to clean up the mess. (The victim recovered and sought out another line of work.)

Both sides in the case had reason to postpone the trial for as long as possible, to interject a demurrer, and so on, giving them time to gather new evidence or to recast the evidence they had in a more advantageous light, to locate additional witnesses or allow the recollections of existing ones to fade a shade in the bright sunlight that existed outside the courtroom. Finally, though, a trial date was set.

In those days the lower courts, municipal and state alike, the places where I first got to know Ostermeyer, were always jammed with minor livewire stuff. I've gone back and looked up the criminal docket for the month that this federal trial was taking place, just to show you how big a deal the Joseph case was by comparison. In terms of the severity of the supposed crime, the hottest non-fed story was a charge of first degree murder against a man, not a full-time professional criminal, in the death of his wife's best friend. In his day the victim had had three indictments against him, but all of them had been nollied. This was a case the reporters were keyed up for, though not to the same extent as they were for United States v. Sells et al. Other matters included a statutory rape; that story would be followed closely because the accused was a talented high school gridder, as sports writers liked to say. Other less dramatic matters that were docketed, and listed here in no special order, included the recapture of a local lamster, bogus payments, false representation, public profanity, public intoxication (many of these), interference with an officer in the execution of his duties, non-support, alienation of affection, and petty larceny. That is to say, it was a normal month in Normal City until a federal judge brought down the opening gavel on the case that promised to go right to the heart and guts of our tranquil community.

Sells, the doorman, and one of the bartenders were

freed on bonds. The second bartender, whose exact nationality was occasionally the subject of conjecture, was free in a different sense. A deputy sheriff trying to serve him with a capias in an unrelated local matter learned that he had left for Europe early the previous morning on a steamship from the port of Baltimore. On the first day of Pete Sells's portion of the trial, two hundred curious citizens elbowed one another for seats in a courtroom that had space for perhaps a quarter that number at most. Once seated, some of the lucky spectators began offering their spots for sale to other eager justice enthusiasts until the judge ordered the bailiff to do his duty and put an end to such nonsense.

A few days later, I have the yellowing clipping in my scrapbook right here in front of me, the *State Journal* startled readers with an instance of editorial prerogative that seemed to have no precedent so far as anyone could remember. On page one, immediately below the image of the stars and stripes on the left ear of the nameplate was a box-rule containing a melodramatic editorial headed THE SHAME OF THE CITY. "The long arm of the Federal Government finally reached out to impede the associates of James (Joseph) Lahoud," the editorial began. "The prospect of ridding the City of this notorious lawbreaker's henchmen is one that will be welcomed by all decent citizens." The article went on to detail the web of municipal and judiciary corruption at the heart of which the supposed "king of the nocturnal underworld" operated. "No self-respecting citizen of the City or this Country can

view the record of the past few years, with all its protected lawlessness, without a feeling of the deepest shame."

Everyone understood that Metzger and the Parthenon
boys were guiding the pen of Clouse figuratively, but this
time there was some other force openly at work—either
that, or Clouse's writing style had certainly changed since
the days of *The Rider*, when wisecracking was in vogue.
I, as a lifelong reader of the local press, suspect that the
above was actually a unique collaboration—forced, or
forged, in anger, who knows? The piece read to me as
pure Metzger: only a lawyer would write that way. I'm
surprised he didn't begin "Whereas…"

The Carpenter must have accumulated another thirty
pounds of gut. As he was no longer comfortable squeezing
behind the steering wheel, he had stopped driving altogether, and a full-time driver was always on call. Through
what Jim couldn't be sure wasn't bulletproof glass (for it
looked kind of funny), his host was pointing out some of
the attractions as the two were being chauffeured to various places of interest. It was the middle of the afternoon.

"La Gauchetière is the main stem of Chinatown. Not
many non-Chinamen have business here, not our kind of
business. They gamble as often as they sit down to eat or
take a drink of water, but it's Chinese gambling. Fan-tan,
tien gow, chee fah. They're the only ones who understand it and the ones controlling it." He smiled. "There
was this what we call a bloke—you know, a dumb English
guy. His wife, she divorced him. He came home drunk in

the middle of the night with a live monkey that he won gambling in Chinatown."

Before the Carpenter could diverge from the topic of Chinatown, Jim brought up the subject of drugs, in what he fancied was his innocent voice, his simple-curiosity voice. The Carpenter pushed a button that raised a glass panel between the driver and the rear seats.

"A lot of older men still kick the gong. That's how they say. But it all comes from China. It's smuggled here and to other Chinese quarters all the way from Vancouver on the West Coast. Opium's a lot more dangerous than most things people do to get along, but it's expensive, because of what you call the soup. I like that expression... But when there are customers, someone will always serve them. Am I not talking the truth?"

"You are, that's for sure."

It was the end of the working day, and the streets of downtown Montreal were full of people who looked too stylishly dressed for wherever they were going. The driver stopped on Drummond Street somewhere. Jim's host led the way across an alley and up two flights of stairs that were difficult for a man of his girth to climb without wheezing like a steam whistle. A man stationed at the top not only recognized him, but seemed alarmed to have such an important personage pass through the door. There was activity from wall to wall, but the hub was a long narrow table, less like the usual craps set-up than like a refectory table in a seminary. Dealers stood at both ends, and gamblers lined up along each side laying down bets and shouting—not professionals but men making their way home from the office. They traded throws. The dice tumbled to a stop and the rollers became faders and the faders became rollers.

"This is what I want you to see. *La barbotte*. It is an old game in Quebec. The players don't bet against the house. They bet against each other." He added, in a boastful whisper, "No Italians and no Irish or anybody else came up with this."

Jim watched the action intently, ignoring the cries of victory and defeat. It didn't take him long to catch on. On the surface the game looked like craps but was more even than that, more back and forth. You won if you rolled 3-3, 5-5, 6-6 or 6-5. You lost if you rolled 1-1, 2-2, 4-4 or 2-1. The amount of money constantly changing hands added up to quite a bundle. Jim was surprised. "I'll be damned."

The Carpenter let loose a hoarse chuckle. "*Les temps sont durs,*" he said, "but this, it goes on no matter." Jim got the gist all right. If American law were to change and the speakeasies disappeared, people might or might not continue to spend what was in their pocket to buy booze to keep them from feeling so sorry for themselves, at least for a little while. But they would certainly gamble on the chance to refill those same pockets. Any winnings that came their way would seem like free money.

The two men watched the play for an hour. "I am the smartest kind of gambler," said the Carpenter. "The kind that does not gamble himself, at least not with his own money." Jim was enjoying his host's wit. "Do not bet against the house. Be the house! But I am breaking my own commandment to teach you the game. You may need to know it in the future when the times come." The Carpenter explained that the house took five cents on a dollar bet, ten cents on three dollars, fifteen cents on ten dollars.

"And more than ten dollars?"

"Ten is the normal limit. This is a game for ordinary people. But sometimes a big shot"—he said the phrase as though it were French—"will buy the room for the evening, then we make a negotiation."

The streets were dark by the time they left. The driver appeared magically, as if by some pre-arranged signal. The passengers piled into their old seats. "I'm going to show you other things you probably haven't seen before. We're going to the southwest of Montreal, between the canal and St. Henri, what the English, the *rosbifs*, call Little Burgundy. La Petite-Bourgogne."

"I think I've been there before, but just wandering around."

The driver took them south down into St. Antoine Ward along funny little streets full of African faces lit up in the glare of signs. Jazz poured out of the buildings. Jim recognized a church he'd seen before, an odd thing with various sizes of cupolas at different levels, each of them topped by a cross. He was beginning to learn his way around. They were getting close to the Lachine Canal.

The thing that you might call the Carpenter's philosophy, especially in difficult times, was to do a little business with the people at the top, a little with the people in the middle, and a little with the ones at the bottom. But he had certain limits, certain cautions. It was unlike him, for instance, to return to a subject he had already finished with. But for the second time that evening, as they drove through the low dark streets he broke one of his rules.

"Some of them here," Jim's host said, "want to bring in the dope." He shook his head. "Maybe a white girl, with *l'esprit aventureux* might try it. When that happens, you have repression." He wagged one of his stubby fingers. "You do not want repression."

Nowadays, he went on, it was the greaseballs who brought the stuff in "from over there or from their cousins in New York." He said "cousins" a special way, making a profanity of it. Was he passing along news or issuing a warning? Jim had no idea. "*Il ne faut pas mettre tous ses œufs dans le même panier.* You have the same expression—not all your eggs in the same basket. It cannot be done that way. Make the big profit from a nice gambling house. Entertain the people." It was suddenly clear to Jim that they were headed for the Carpenter's own establishment. "Attract the men with big money from St. James Street who need a little sin every once and a while. The word gets out. Players come up from the big places in the States. Men who like to gamble ten or twelve hours in a row. You see? But what are we doing for the other people? *La barbotte.* The track. And down at the bottom end, the numbers. You have the numbers where you are?"

"Not me. But somebody does. It's mostly the Negroes."

"Ah, well, there you have an opportunity, my young friend. The numbers are to be the thing, you wait and see. *Je suis un prophète, moi*, you'll see!" He didn't laugh often or carelessly, but when he did it was like a sound coming up from the cellar.

A few moments later, the Carpenter gave the chauffeur the signal to pull over. Both men disembarked. The host clambered out with some difficulty, and spoke a few words to the driver.

"So this is your Harlem." Jim spoke the obvious.

"More and more, believe me. And it will be hot! You see, thirty years ago, maybe longer, the railways started hiring the black people to be everything from porters to redcaps. First they brought them over the border. Then Canadian Negroes, some from as far away as Halifax on the Atlantic Ocean, were given jobs also. Now we're beginning to see ones from the Caribbean, mostly English from Jamaica, but some French too from Haiti and other places. All these people wanted to be near their work, near Windsor Station. They made homes up and down these streets. This is where jazz came to town."

Standing where they were, the men could hear proof of this fact coming at them through the windows and the cracks of old buildings. If he turned around in a circle, Jim could probably have seen a dozen different joints lit up like Christmas trees.

"You see that stylish gentleman near the door up there?" They were standing close to the corner of Craig and Mountain streets. "He's a numbers runner. People like him run around all day and afternoon picking up bets from people, as small as a penny and big as a dollar or two. He gives them slips—their receipts. Then, somewhere in this city the policy bankers have to sort out what the three numbers for the day are. And the bankers send their runners out again to give the winners what they have won."

"As I said, I've always heard about the numbers, but I don't know much about it."

"You should learn, my friend. Simple as it sounds, this lottery brings huge amounts of money with only a little work—a lot of organizing, but only a little real work. Right now, this game is played only in the dark parts of Montreal, though you have to wonder who really runs it. Imagine if white people begin to like it big time. I think this might be ready to happen. All those white clubs uptown that have black entertainment. You'll see the advertising for them. So and So and His Harlem Gentlemen, or Somebody Else and the High-Steppin' Something or Others. You see them all the time, playing for white audiences. The white people seem to like the old-fashioned names. More and more, the people from Westmount and everywhere else want to be coming down here instead in their good autos, wearing tuxedos and diamonds. Many times they start out at dinner somewhere else but then come along here when the hour gets late. They're learning the difference between Paul Whiteman and real jazz, the kind that picks you up and leaves you to sweat. I think this is making a bigger audience for the numbers."

"You're a wise man."

"No, I just mind my own business, but my ears and eyes stay open."

The Carpenter's own club was called the Grotto. It was a tony place on the top two floors of an otherwise undistinguished three-storey building. There was a tall vertical sign with a green palm tree on top. A Negro, a big strong fellow, was the doorman. He wore harem trousers and some kind of Arab vest, and had a curved sword in the Arab style but made of wood, the blade painted grey to suggest steel or silver. The house was packed. Some whites, some of them French, but mostly Negroes.

The moment the two men entered, everything seemed to stop. Were they were surprised because the boss didn't usually enter through the front door? Jim wondered, not for the first time, about the Carpenter's habits.

The man who seemed to be the manager showed them to a particularly roomy booth. "How are we doing this evening, sir?" he asked. The Carpenter ordered them drinks in French. On the opposite wall was the most magnificent bar set-up Jim had ever seen. Except for the top surface, the bar was made of metal. The stools were actually tall chairs, upholstered in black leather. Behind the bar, everything was glass. Lights behind that, set right into the wall, invisibly emitted pastel light that filtered through the various gins, scotches, bourbons, vodkas and rums making the wall itself a kaleidoscopic display. The barmen were slim with slicked hair; their short white jackets were immaculate and heavily starched. They seemed to speak every language at par and without fuss.

Overlooking the booths were framed eight-by-ten photographs of performers and celebrities, both black and white. The closest one Jim could make out was inscribed, with a clumsy flourish, "To Leonard the dean of Montreal from his friend Louis."

The Carpenter was watching Jim's reaction. "Acts like that play at those places downtown. They sign contracts that keep them from appearing anywhere else in the city. I guess I can see the hotels' point of view. They deal out a good deal of money after all. But people like Louis Armstrong, all the big names, come in here when they finish their shows. Sometimes they will play all together in the room upstairs. Always late at night, always until near morning."

"Leonard is the guy who came over when we first sat down?"

The Carpenter lowered his voice, though the room was noisy. "Leonard speaks very good English as you heard, but he's from the Martinique. He is a one of a kind. You see, there was a time when the city did not like to give a liquor permit to a Negro. But I was able to reason with some people I know at the City Hall. The place is his." The last sentence was spoken in the harmless tone of a fib.

At the back of the room, one of the swinging doors to the kitchen flung open and a Negro chef approached Leonard. He was wearing a tall puffy chef's hat, which resembled some grand pastry he probably knew how to make. He spoke French with great agitation. Leonard replied calmly, and seemed to smooth out whatever the problem was.

"Funny how life works," Jim said. "If my family hadn't gone to the United States when they did, I could be speaking French right now."

"Why is that?"

"It's been almost ten years since France took over Lebanon. This was a big issue in my part of town, you might imagine."

"Yes," said the Carpenter. "It is a sad thing to happen."

"Ah, there's sadder things." He lifted his glass, and the Carpenter raised his in turn.

Allan Ostermeyer:

I think Pete's trial caused another rift between him and his partner. Or maybe it had already begun with the speculation that they were arguing about money. Pete thought he was being shortchanged. There is a maxim we learned in law school. *Ex nudo pacto non oritur actio.* Or, translated into Pete's patois: "The contract ain't legit if no dough changes hands."

As for the drama in the courtroom, opinion in the gaming and gossip fraternities was all over the map. No one much cared what happened to the doorman and the remaining bartender, but everyone had a hunch, a notion, a suspicion, a belief or a piece of inside information about the fate of Pete Sells. Would he beat the rap? If so, would the crookedness of the judge be the deciding factor? Might the prosecutor suddenly vacate the case, possibly on evidentiary grounds? Could the matter end with a hung jury, legitimately or otherwise? Or would Sells simply be convicted? If so, could McConnell's lawyers find grounds for an appeal? The bookmakers were beside themselves. To the surprise of many, the trial was quite speedy: Pete was found guilty and sentenced to two years. The two other defendants scraped by with six months each.

The period between the sentencing and the prisoners surrendering for transportation proved longer than expected. The judge had initially sentenced Pete to the Atlanta penitentiary, but with weeks to go there was a serious outbreak of meningitis in the institution. For the moment, no new inmates were being accepted, and a number of existing convicts were transferred temporarily to the prison at Petersburg, Virginia. In the meantime, there was plenty of time for Jim to plan a big farewell dinner for his brother-in-law in an expensive restaurant taken over for the occasion. Those attending included two entire roast lambs, the pastor of Our Lady of Lebanon, the mayor, the police chief, three-fourths of the city council, and a good proportion of the city's most prominent liquor men, gamblers, and nocturnal worthies. There were no reporters. Nor, it being mostly a stag affair, were there many women—and only one decent one, Thidi McConnell. She and the evening's VIP argued loudly the entire time. She had had a great deal to drink when she was accustomed to very little and at one point screamed at Pete in a stage whisper audible to all, "Get your goddamned hand off my thigh, you hoodlum!" He replied that she was a rich bitch and slapped her across the face, and she grabbed her evening bag and fled. After that, some of the warm encomiums being offered to Pete from the podium sounded a bit hollow. Jim was sad, in a furious way. Over the next few days, the two men talked about their joint business interests and what was to be done during Pete's absence. Obviously resentful that he was taking the rap, Pete was difficult to handle. Jim hoped—knew—that life would be more orderly while his partner was away, but two years wasn't a long time. Jim dreaded what would happen when Pete got sprung.

The following week, Pete was escorted to the railway station. The week after that, the New York stock exchange collapsed like a three-legged chair.

In the liquor trade just as in the legitimate population, several schools of thought emerged in the rapidly spreading series of calamities that followed. Many figured, or believed, thought, hoped, or prayed, that the financial panic was temporary, similar to the dip in '21 or the recession the elderly remembered from '93. There were even some still living who had suffered in the panic of '76. At least a few among the bootlegging professionals looked on the news every day with mounting certainty that they had made the right decision in getting into some other racket, or at least adding a few sidelines, not only because the federal government was really cracking down, but also because, with so many out of work, the market for booze would shrink almost to nothing. There were also men such as Pete. From his cell he let people know that he wanted to keep going as though nothing was the matter. Such stubbornness brought on another fight with Jim, this one through a mesh screen after Zelfa had finished her allotted time with her brother. She was praying, she had told him, for his safety.

A second boiling point was reached on a subsequent visit. Jim, having rehearsed what he was going to say until he had it down pat, warned him to stop seeing McConnell's daughter once his sentence was up.

"McConnell's mad as hell," Joseph said.

"Yeah, well, she doesn't live under his roof anymore."

"Well, don't let her hang around under yours. Look around you. The world's full of flappers if that's your taste. For God's sake be careful. Very careful."

Pete didn't take the suggestion well. Years later Jim would say that, ludicrous as it sounded, he thought for half a second that his brother-in-law might pull out of his waistband a pistol he had had someone smuggle in. Fortunately, the flare-up, though hot, was also short, and ended when talk turned once again, as it did most of the time now, to the economic emergency. According to Jim, they were in a position to start putting their new business plans into play, and look at using money from the sale of the bootlegging enterprise to make money, like intelligent businessmen. He also gave Pete the latest gossip from back home: the *Inter-Ocean* had been taken over by the *Enterprise*, which people were saying wouldn't be long for this world either. Pete just shrugged.

Edwin Staffel:

Economics notwithstanding, the city to which Pete returned, after serving only sixteen months of his sentence, had been peaceful for almost a year and a half.

Every Sunday morning, Jim drove Zelfa to Our Lady. Theirs was an affectionate relationship, indeed a loving one, but Americans didn't always understand this when they saw Jim driving and her sitting, as she still insisted on doing, in the back seat, like the dignified Lebanese lady she was. On the important religious holidays Jim would accompany her to church. At other times, she attended alone. She always took quiet comfort in the four spots during Mass where the priest uttered several phrases in Aramaic. She enjoyed thinking that she was listening to the language actually spoken by Jesus. Jim, parked a few blocks away behind the Sons of Lebanon Benevolent Society, sipped strong syrupy coffee and picked up news of who was in difficulties, who had taken ill, who had found work at last (there weren't many of these), who had had another baby. After church, husband and wife talked as they drove all the way back to the Rose Apartments, past the hobo jungle already taking shape under the abutments of the High Level Bridge. Zelfa mentioned other news of people's families—people they knew and people they didn't: the kind of information that women pass among themselves when men aren't around. But she never spoke about Pete. Jim didn't know whether she felt humiliated and ashamed, or perhaps just plain sad.

Zelfa would ask her husband when all this was going to stop so they could have a normal life, though it wasn't so much an actual question, or even a complaint or a request, as a wish, possibly a prayer. Now Jim could see that it was becoming a last straw, one he had to deal with, just as he had dealt with Pete. Zelfa was clearly agitated one evening when Jim picked her up at the Our Lady of Lebanon annex following the monthly meeting of the ladies' auxiliary, where she sat on the ways-and-means committee and where she had always been listened to respectfully and with deference. Jim could sense that something was amiss even before she started to speak from the back seat. The tone of the meeting had taken a sharp turn and started to unravel when some of the members, whose high regard for Zelfa had perhaps been a product of their hidden fear, failed to keep their feelings under wraps any longer. The auxiliary had voted down Zelfa's proposal to donate funds to establish a free soup-and-sandwich program for poor children living in or near the Triangle. They approved of the idea but told her in unsubtle terms that they didn't want the church accepting dirty money.

One Monday shortly thereafter, Jim pulled his car up outside a small frame house on Decatur Street deep in the Triangle. A handwritten sign on the front door directed people to go around to the side. Jim did so and knocked, then knocked again. Street kids were beginning to point at the swell automobile with the side curtains. The door opened and Jim took off his hat. "Mrs. Ballouz, my name is James Joseph. You may remember me from Our Lady."

The woman in a worn cotton housedress was non-plussed. "Oh, everybody knows who you are," she said.

"May I come in?"

"Please. Yes."

The screen door slammed shut behind him as he stepped into the kitchen. The two of them settled into mismatched second-hand chairs. The only decoration on the walls was a lithograph of President Roosevelt cut out of a magazine. A radio buzzed in another room. Jim knew the Ballouz girl was housebound, and probably confined to her bed, for that matter.

"My wife..."

"A fine lady, yessir."

"...has told me about your troubles."

"I'll tell you honest, Mr. Joseph, I could have gotten through this when Tom was alive, but now, with no money coming in..." Her voice began to waver, and she straightened up in her chair.

"I'm sorry to hear about your situation, and I'd like you to take this. It's the name of a surgeon who will operate on your daughter. The telephone number is right there on the card. I've looked into the matter, and I'm told he's a brilliant physician. If anybody can help, he can."

She seemed overwhelmed. "Well, I don't know what..."

"The doctor's fees are already taken care of. Mrs. Joseph and I will continue to pray for a happy outcome."

As Jim picked up his hat to leave, the older woman began to weep.

Finally and at long last, on December 5th of 1933, the Twenty-first Amendment to the Constitution was ratified, eliminating the Eighteenth, and Prohibition was finished. The universe would soon change as a result. One era was over, and all of a sudden the world was different from whatever it had been so recently. What had been the present was now the past, and therefore easy to figure out. Smart men had seen it coming, and had prepared themselves.

Everybody had made money from bootlegging. That was the beauty of the business, but also the problem with it. It was too much of a free-for-all. Big money people brought booze down from Canada. It had been an especially good time to be a Canadian. Anyone could get rich without too much risk, because how the buyers got it into the United States was their problem. Some bigwigs even brought in good stuff from Scotland, which, once safely landed, was usually diluted, though it was still branded as the real McCoy. Nobody needed much capital to begin. This was the era of the big bootleggers of the headlines, who were always getting a bigger and bigger slice by acquiring their competitors one way or another—acquiring their production or their customers, or both. Big business is always dirty business.

Every Joe knew of such people. We in the press gave them lurid nicknames. But more than that, and on a homemade scale, this was the time of grain alcohol and food dye, local leggers, and immigrant mamas using rug beaters and soup ladles to stir up recipes they'd come up with on their own. Yes, gin in bathtubs, not to mention the heavy lead stationary tubs used for rinsing clothes on washday before putting them through the wringer. And it didn't stop there. These were boom times for those who owned a truck or two or whose business was making glass bottles—or for kids who collected used ones from alleyways, vacant lots, and dumps. Nearly bankrupt cooperages came alive again. There was suddenly a steady demand for more corks! It was a complex business even at the ma-and-pa level. The closer an ambitious person such as Jim got to the top, even just locally, the more maddening every day became, the more money he made, the more he had to spend in order to keep what he had. The harder he worked, the more time he had to spend in the company of lawyers. At one point, Jim had almost as many lawyers as Pete Sells had automobiles, for he was arrested a couple more times, though never seriously—fined or nollied, charges dropped, raps beaten, except during the mayoralty race when he'd spent a little time in jail. As Mr. Clouse once told his editorial people, "Joseph, that son of a bitch, has no convictions except the ones he gets overturned on appeal." At such moments, Clouse considered himself a wit.

This disparity in the fates of the Jim Joseph and Pete Sells left Sells with a permanent grudge against Jim—another one.

The original idea was to celebrate Pete's release (rather than his rehabilitation, for there was none of that) by asking him along on a little vacation to Montreal. He'd never been there, not even briefly, though that hadn't prevented him from badmouthing the place to Jim, as though cities were women and the poor ones envied the rich ones and were jealous. Jim thought his partner needed to relax, seeing that he'd just got out of the jute farm, where relaxation was unknown, and not merely because it was forbidden.

Jim was not without guile in trying to bring Pete around to the idea of a trip. "Look, I've tried to explain this to you. We've talked about moving downtown and opening a new place. I want you to take a look at the Grotto, our friend's layout up there."

"And I keep telling you that that's the stupidest idea I've ever heard. You've gotta be bats. People are lining up in the streets for food. The mills are down to two shifts. Soon they'll be down to one. The way it looks to me, everybody's business is just barely hanging on. What's that do to us, when our business is making them spend money with us, and they got no money?"

This became an ongoing argument. Jim too saw the people without work—how could you miss the poor buggers?—the men and women without the energy to hope any longer. Sure, business was off at the Paddock and the Roosevelt (as the Allies had been tactfully renamed). But the answer was to compensate for the fall-off by bringing in high rollers from other cities, from all over this part of the country, and maybe even beyond. They still existed all right and always would. McConnell could be a great help there. Millionaires all seemed to know one another, even when they were rivals and enemies, even when one of them was McConnell, known locally if mistakenly as the world's only millionaire Democrat.

But the real lift would come from the Carpenter. The Montreal Italians and Greeks, they were all tied in to New York. They would never let the Carpenter into their rackets because he was a frog, part of the frog majority, so he had become an expert at prospering without them. He fixed things, he made things happen; he exemplified the high style even while cultivating people like Pete and Jim, helping them out, these characters nobody else in Montreal ever heard of, maybe one day selling them a local sub-franchise to the race wire, who knows? All sorts of things were possible. Jim Joseph was quick to get the message. Make sure you're connected, and more and more people will stick to you. So will the coins in their pockets.

Allan Ostermeyer:

Jim stopped one morning, as he liked doing, to get the early papers from Blind Billy who ran the tiny cigar stand in the lobby of the Tontine Building. Billy had a phenomenal memory not only for the voices and footsteps of his customers but also for figures. As Pete once put it, "It's well the Good Lord has made it up to him for the loss of his sight. Otherwise he couldn't make change and wouldn't be any goddamn good in the numbers." Billy took in people's bets, and gave them slips as receipts.

Under his counter there was a row of small bowls from a chop-suey joint. Combined with his memory, the bowls were like an adding machine. When somebody laid a quarter on, say, 623, he would slowly, in big round numerals, write out the figure on a little slip of paper and put his personal mark at the bottom. Then he would move pebbles from one bowl to another to have a record of the transaction that he can read with his fingers. If the customer, trying to impress his girl, paid a little more and told Billy to "box it," he would also get the payoff if the number 326 came up instead of 623, and in that case Billy made a second mark, a special one. Jim was always kind to Blind Billy, one of the scores of people on his list to get a free turkey at Christmas.

"What time does the runner come by?" Jim asked.

Three o'clock, Blind Billy said. Jim told Pete to send one of his guys to stake out the place, discreetly, from across the street, follow him to wherever all the slips were taken, and report back.

"That's stupid," Sells said. "Why not just ask the blind guy and pick him up by his black ears if he won't answer?"

Working with Pete Sells had forced Jim to cultivate a certain degree of patience.

"Let's do it my way," he said. Pete shrugged his broad shoulders, blew on the diamond he wore on the third finger of his right hand and shot the cuffs of his custom-made shirt. "Okey-dokey."

The trail of the numbers runner, another Negro, led to a little unmarked building. Pete's fellow, the same white man who had tried to blend in at the pre-election rally at the Negro Knights of Pythias nearby, waited outside, counting the men who came and went. They never stayed long. With the address of the building, it was easy to learn the owner's identity. Pete's thug got a look at the fellow when he left; he was one of the radicals who had complained about not being paid the same as Caucasians for voting. He shadowed him home and got his name. Nothing about the fellow or where he resided suggested that he was doing well in the lottery business.

Jim used George Taggart to arrange a meeting on neutral ground. Jim knew how small the operation was, and he also knew it got clipped by the cops every so often. The opening asking price was two grand. There was quite a bit of back and forth. In the end, Jim offered fifteen hundred dollars in cash and one percent of the profits in the first year, falling to zero in the second and thereafter. He promised to keep on any of the writers and runners who wanted to stay. A white hand and a black hand clasped and shook.

The numbers were the answer—the numbers, and barbut, or barbooty (Americans didn't know how to pronounce the word and so even the newspapers spelled it a number of different ways). These two games looked like the future, or part of it.

Every city where people played the numbers seemed to use a different method of selecting the winning digits. In many places, in the Midwest especially, policy bosses would look at the business pages of the evening papers to see the total value processed that day at an institution called the Cincinnati Clearing House. (Why Cincinnati? No one seemed to know. There were so many who didn't trust the system.) It was a figure somewhere in the millions of dollars. The last digit of the dollar figure and the two figures to the right of the decimal point together were the winning number. Periodically some Clearing House employee would be accused of rigging the outcome somehow. But most places took the matter into their own hands, which opened the way for shady operators. That is to say, human nature being what it is, somebody was always trying to put the fix in. Even in joints where they rolled ten-sided dice, some joker would be accused of injecting them with mercury to increase the odds of getting his own lucky number to come up. Less fancy places chose numbered balls out of a big round spinning cage—like bingo, which was also considered a crime in those days. Most seemed to prefer three chuck-a-luck set-ups in sequence, drawing one numbered ball from each cage to make up the winning trio.

The arrangement at the Paddock was the usual, but always top-end. Three cages on a baize-covered table. The special dice were red, yellow, and blue. A volunteer from the gathered crowd would spin his cage and pull out a number, then two other fellows did the same. The three numbers were right there on the table for everyone to see (but not to touch) and that combination was proclaimed the winner. Men working a bank of telephones along the back wall would begin calling the middlemen to give them the result.

This operetta had two shows daily. The payouts from the afternoon roll were made at night, and those from the evening roll, the following morning. Some fools and self-proclaimed big shots put up a little folding money, as much as $25 or $30, but most bet pennies, nickels, dimes, quarters, even, dare it be said, a half dollar. It was a cop-per-and-silver business, to be sure but, since it was within the budget of absolutely everybody, even the beggars on street corners, the numbers game was astonishingly lucra-tive, certainly so for the men at the top, but also for a few of the bettors. The winners were rewarded at six hun-dred to one, less ten per cent paid to the writers. So if you bet one cent and won, you'd receive six dollars less sixty cents, or $5.40 net.

Such wagers soon became everybody's obsession. Or-dinary people—secretaries, street cleaners, mechanics, garbage collectors, schoolteachers, billiard-hall layabouts, everybody but preachers—bet incessantly, all of them day after day, some of them putting down two or three bets over the course of a morning or an afternoon. Everybody had a lucky number, or so he thought. Those who couldn't conjure one up all by themselves—this applied most of-ten to women from one Old Country or another—would reach for the dog-eared dream book that hung by a string from a nail on the kitchen wall. If the previous night they had dreamt of, say, a lion or a burning house, they had only to look up "lion" or "burning house" and find the number that corresponded to that image. Who knew? It must have worked at least once in a blue moon. No one ever broke the bank. But there were two days that first year when payments exceeded what came in. In the worse instance, when the gross take was $1,899.06, the night roll turned up the magic number 501. A variety of different citizens had bet a total of $6.95 on that number, mostly in pennies and nickels. So the house paid out $4,170. The other day was far worse. "Days like this are good for business," Jim assured Pete and their ever-growing band of employees. "Word gets around of a big strike and people start feeling they'll be the lucky ones next time."

"Don't worry."

Edwin Staffel:

"I don't like having another partner." Pete was gunning for what sounded like the beginning of another of their disagreements. "Kasdan. What the hell kind of name is that? Sounds Persian."

"No, he's a Jew."

Sells snorted. "And that's supposed to be better?"

"And he's not a partner the way the two of us are partners. He works for us and he works damned hard. He earns what we pay him."

"You mean what he pays himself."

"Well, he is the bookkeeper, so yeah, he writes 'em and I sign 'em."

Of course, matters were much more complicated than that, so complicated that Kasdan felt hopeless at first in trying to decode what was actually taking place.

The business was growing so fast that it now took up two suites of offices, one above the Paddock and another in the Roosevelt. Sells was in charge of building up the roster of ticket-writers and runners. With so many out of work and needing a few extra dollars, this proved simpler than he had imagined. In a remarkably short time it seemed every bartender, bellhop, elevator boy, soda jerk, and gasoline jockey in the city was signed up. Buying and selling booze had turned Sells into a pretty good organizer. No doubt his talent for threatening people helped as well.

When a cigar-store clerk or men's room attendant took a customer's bet, he wrote it in a numbers book that had two sheets of carbon paper attached. He'd give the top copy to the bettor, put one aside for the runner (sometimes called a pick-up man) and retained the third for his own records should a dispute arise. The betting slips were sorted under the suspicious eyes of Sells and his friends, observed by any bettor who craved suspense and excitement or just wanted to see how the process worked.

There was simply too much cash lying around, with overflow from the two safes stuffed in drawers and hidden in cubbyholes. Jim sent Kasdan to one of the banks to open two new accounts, one in the name of Joseph Knighton, the other in the name of Peter S. Day. Poor Kasdan was more than willing to do so, though he sighed. Here he was, charged with bringing order to his two bosses' various enterprises, and these people were mostly using cash, even for salaries; receipts, when any existed, tended to be mere notes, scribbled in pencil on matchbooks, cocktail napkins, and corners of pages torn out of the *Racing Form*. Kasdan asked Jim for an accounting of what was in the big safe. He had to nag but finally, as he happened to pass by, he spotted Jim counting bundles of old bills. The next day, Jim whispered in Kasdan's ear: "About two hundred thirty-six thousand and change, more or less." But where did it come from and what was it for? "Savings," Jim said. "Savings and miscellaneous. Though some of it I may be holding for a friend."

Kasdan was not easily exasperated. He took charge of every single piece of paper with writing or figures on it and got Jim's okay to interview everyone connected to the businesses. He initiated new systems, with daily, weekly, and monthly totals of what came in and from whom, and of what went out and for what. The job took months, but at length he was able to make his report to Messrs. Knighton and Day, imperfect and inexact though the tallies obviously were.

"There are two sets of books," he began. "There's what I call the dry ledger, which you gentlemen might wish to use in speaking with your tax accountant."

"You're our tax accountant," Sells said. "Now it's official."

Kasdan cleared his throat and continued. "And there is what I shall call the wet ledger, which, as your past record keeping has been so, shall we say, informal, is the best I can do though it's bound to entail a certain amount of conjecture."

Pete scowled, but Jim raised his eyebrows. "Okay, so what did you find?"

"Well, here goes. Here's how it breaks down. The soup is averaging $3,928.90 a month. Does that sound too high to you or too low?"

Jim and Pete looked at each other. The former answered for both of them. "That's just in the city, you know. No soup for the state people." He smiled at Sells who smirked back. "And none for the feds."

Kasdan resumed. "So, a cost of doing business." He then went through commissions and wages, repairs to buildings and equipment, and gasoline, oil, and maintenance for the automobiles (there were now thirty-six taxis, though the cab business was just a minor sideline by this time). "There are other categories that seem a bit out of the ordinary. What are 'overlooked hits'? I found a note with that phrase and a figure—it's hard to make it out clearly: $1,196."

"Sometimes," Jim said, "a customer doesn't twig to the fact that he had a win until a day or two have gone by. We pay out anyway. It's a small amount of money to avoid trouble and not get badmouthed all over town."

"Then you have 'bad debts' and fees—I don't know what the fees are—totalling $311.15."

"Again, small potatoes."

"And 'money stolen'?"

"We had those two raids, remember? The cops haven't given back the evidence yet." He added, as an afterthought, "I'll adjust the soup."

Kasdan continued. "So is that related to 'employees arrested', which I assume refers to fines? Quite a larger sum: $3,224.78."

"'Cost of doing business.' I like that expression you use."

"And what are 'Montreal special tickets'?"

Sells interrupted. "Don't get him started on Montreal! We'll be here all night."

Jim ignored the remark and told Kasdan to tell them the big number that all this was leading up to.

Kasdan took a deep breath. "You don't have figures for all of the first quarter, as you know. I didn't start until March. But between March third and December thirty-first, you deposited $721,745.31 in various banks and in the two safes. That's all lottery money. It doesn't include barbett or whatever it's called or the various other sources of revenue." Amazing.

The problem with the numbers was not only that some of the public thought that the policy was fixed, but also that rival hoodlums kept calling one another crooks as they tried to make inroads into the other fellow's territory. Soon there would be real trouble. It would be like the legging business all over again. Somebody had to bring order to the racket. Who would have guessed that the solution to this new American problem would come from north of the border?

Although he was wasn't much known outside Montreal, except by those who had done business there,

Monsieur Charpentier was a genius of sorts. As with ge-
niuses generally, his best ideas seemed astoundingly simple, and people wondered why they themselves hadn't
come up with them in the first place. There was that fellow in New York named Rothstein. Nobody liked him,
as I understand it, which is no doubt why he was shot to
death in a hotel on West 56th Street, though everyone admitted his brilliance in rigging the 1919 World Series and,
what's more, getting away with it. The Carpenter's genius
was different. Those who know these things say that he
was the person who figured out that the policy books had
to run as smoothly as the stock market, and in fact should
feed off the stock market. It was him—this is the truth, or
at least the legend—who came up with the idea of using
the last three digits of the total number of shares traded
every day on the New York Stock Exchange. Every afternoon the bell rang, trading stopped, and there, in a few
minutes, you had the big winning number. Everybody,
no matter where they were, got the same three numbers
at the same instant as everybody else. It was on the radio, it was going through the telegraph wires, it was in
the late-afternoon editions of the papers. No one could
ever pretend to predict what it was going to be. No one
was able to fix it. This put an end to night rolls and day
rolls, for there could be only one call every twenty-four
hours. But there were benefits: trust was introduced into
the operation, suspicion declined, violence was prevented
or at least reduced. The exchange was closed on Sunday,
but when someone asked Jim about this, he answered,

"the man in Montreal is religious too." Then there was Christmas Day, and the Fourth of July, and so on. But gamblers and rounders need their rest like everybody else.

From the diary of Cynthia McConnell:

I'm writing this from the Caroline Apartments. Two days have gone by and I haven't really unpacked yet; most of my things are still spread out all over. I'm lucky to have found this diary, though long dormant, because I need something to scribble in. I find it a handy medium for rage. Father called me in for one of his talks and told me how angry he was with Jim Joseph for ignoring his repeated demands to keep Pete and me apart. He really let go, telling me that I was ruining my life—and his, and Mother's. The word "disgrace" was uttered. So was the word "gangster," which made me laugh in his face. I said that, unlike him, I wasn't interested in how Pete made his money, that at least he earned it instead of inheriting it, and that he and I had fun. The rough talk went back and forth, and some of my words came from all the way down in my stomach somewhere. I was franker than I meant to be, certainly franker than I should have been, and in what became a very hot argument I let him know, without actually giving away details, that I was crazy about Pete. I said I was rejecting all this criticism of him and me.

The atmosphere got so bad in that damned den that I can't even remember how long I was there. Without using the exact words, Father finally threatened to boot me out of his will if I didn't immediately stop "dating" Pete. That made me so mad I

could barely see. My body was shaking. I said I didn't really care
a hoot about his will, but I must have sounded as though I did
when I called him a blackmailer. He responded by calling me a
very nasty and degrading term that no man, let alone a father,
should ever utter. I yelled that I was leaving for good. Hedy overheard some of this—how could she not?—and when I ran into her
on the upstairs landing I could see she was very upset. When I'd
thrown in enough clothes and such to fill two suitcases and a valise
I asked her to call me a cab. It was a C. & J. I guess that shouldn't
have surprised me. After all Pete and his partner still owned the
company, which had become by far the biggest in town, as Pete
(Pete and his love of automobiles!) had forced out or bought up
nearly all the competition. I went straight to his suite.

There was no answer at his door. It was locked, but I had a
key and I knew he never put the chain on. The driver had helped
me up with the bags and I left them in the corridor for the moment
and went looking for the one man I thought could help me to calm
down and see things clearly. I passed through the anteroom, the
sitting room and the dining room and finally went to the bedroom.
The door wasn't shut and there he was in bed with a woman,
making love. He turned red with embarrassment and I turned red
with something else. The flapper or prostitute or whatever she was
(it's hard to tell when somebody's naked) looked startled, dazed,
and pulled one of the sheets up over most of herself. Pete—I can
barely make my fingers write these words—looked me straight in
the eye and said, with a big smile: "What's cookin'? Why don't
you hop in? There's plenty of room." The next second he hiked his
shoulders all of a sudden, as though a very mild electrical current
had passed through him, and then sniffed hard with both nostrils.

On his nightstand, next to his gun, was a single-edge razor blade and a tiny pyramid of bright white powder, no higher than your little finger is wide. I saw that the girl had some white residue just above her lip, something like a child with a white moustache from drinking milk. He saw me looking at the table, then at her, then back at him. "Lots of tix here," he said. "Hell, we had a whole deck goin' for us. Ain't that right, babe?" The girl didn't answer.

I was mortified and for a moment I thought I was about to collapse. I bounced my luggage down to the entrance at street level and went off to first find another taxi. And a new place to live.

Edwin Staffel:

Most people would have laughed if you told them that Jim Joseph was a champion of law and order. That's just one of the things the public misunderstood about him, but compared with his brother-in-law, he was. The cops were getting theirs every month on the basis of seniority; there was a fixed sum for roundsmen, another for sergeants, lieutenants, and captains, yes even captains, an arrangement run smooth as silk by Kasdan and what had become his stable of abacus-flippers. But the recipients of the envelopes started getting greedy in their new prosperity. I guess they figured since they were taking money from Jim Joseph they might as well turn thief themselves. But not Jim. If he cut the soup, they could always blow the whole racket to a grand jury. The whole operation could go down the drain if the city administration ever changed. These cops were prudent, careful people, like Jim himself. They knew better than to try and rinse him. Instead they made extra money stealing from merchants. Some brazen cops would just pull up to, for instance, a radio store downtown, and take away some Philcos and Magnavoxes as supposed evidence. The shopkeeper wouldn't complain, not after the first time. He would come to accept that this was a cost of doing business without getting hurt. This stuff happened all over town. I once saw a prowl car with a brand-new sofa tied to the roof, sticking out a few feet over the rear: evidence for some copper's living room. What they did not need they laid off with a fence.

But the cops went too far, and eventually the retail trade started turning against them and began pushing Jim to do something. It took some doing, but Jim got young Nolte made the chief—the youngest one in the history of the force, jumping all the way from sergeant of detectives in one bound. Not everyone was happy at this, especially the Fraternal Order of Police, but Jim got it pushed through. And this is how I got my big break. There's no predicting something like this. Sometimes you're lucky. It just happens.

I was still a relatively young reporter in 1936, not wet behind the ears but quite full of myself, and I detested the police beat. Police headquarters in the basement of the old red stone City Hall included a small pressroom, just a desk and one or two chairs. There were out-of-date girlie calendars and tobacco stains on the walls where, I imagine, cops, rather than reporters, had spat, to show their contempt for us. There was also a hole in the ceiling, said to have been caused by a bullet fired years earlier by a disgruntled old cop named Brockhart.

I don't know what Mr. Clouse thought about the cops working on their own account. I suppose he was against it even though it was free enterprise. But he was a very conservative man, more and more so as he got older. The *Register* always referred to gambling as gaming. "The local gaming community...." In his paper, Clouse forbade the word. It was gambling. Gambling was a sin and should be presented for what it was, not prettied up as though it were something fit for the schoolyard.

There had been a number of claims of police roughing up shopkeepers and also Negroes, the latter presumably just for laughs. In such cases there were always conflicting eyewitness accounts and the results would come out inconclusively when somebody got scared. As one of the new guys at the paper, I had a terrible shift, two p.m. to midnight, Tuesday through Sunday. City Hall was four blocks from the paper.

One morning I got a call from the city desk saying that a pair of priests at St. Mike's said that they were looking out the chancery window when they saw two cops rob an old black man and then beat him until he was a bloody pulp and couldn't rise up. Thereupon they kicked him in the head several times for good measure and took him to jail. The witnesses were shocked, but they weren't frightened in the least, and they offered to be interviewed about what they had seen. I stopped by to see them on my way to work. At the back of my mind, and at the back of Mr. Clouse's, I figured, was the thought that this might be the break needed to bust open Jim's failure to control the cop machine he had created. These were priests, after all, coming forward without apparent fear. They didn't have any motive for dissembling, not that we could think of anyway. They were credible and spoke on the record. The trouble was they didn't have any details beyond what they had witnessed, though they were certainly graphic about what they saw. At one point, they told me, as I wrote as quickly as I could, the two cops were bashing the poor Negro's head as hard as they could against the hood ornament of a Pontiac parked at the curb—a big metal Indian head. But they didn't know why the victim was singled out, unless it was just a racial matter. They didn't have his name or the identity of the two patrolmen or knowledge of what, if anything, aside from just existing, the victim had done to prompt the attack. As soon as I got back to the paper I was sent to the police station, feeling tremendous pressure from the city room, and what the city room represented, to nail the thing down.

Word had quickly gotten out that perhaps this incident was going to be a black eye for the department, a real shiner, and that no piece of beefsteak was going to reduce the swelling. Since the last election a few years earlier, racial temperatures had been running high. No one wanted a race riot like those erupting here and there across the country, both north and south. Chief Nolte was promising an internal investigation but refused to say whether the results would be made public (I guessed they wouldn't be—and they weren't, not by him at least). Over the next few weeks everyone was tense as the city waited for the whitewash. Everywhere I went in the police department even those who'd normally been somewhat helpful gave me the cold shoulder. "Oh, nothing's available on that." "The chief is looking into it." "No information will be forthcoming for another week." Cops, secretaries—everybody—gave me the same brush-off.

One day, as the afternoon was drawing to a close and the deadline for the four-star edition was nearing, I was increasingly concerned about what Mr. Clouse would do if I showed up back at the paper again with nothing but further observations by the priests and excuses from the cops. Failure hung over me like a scimitar. I was absolutely deflated and dejected, thinking I had struck out completely and fearing what would become of me, my career cut short.

My last resort was to go upstairs to the jail and try to talk my way into the log of recently admitted inmates, and perhaps figure out a name and a charge that matched the poor victim who was being kept incommunicado, which would involve a lot of guesswork and a hostile jailer no doubt. Without much confidence, I headed to the elevator, an old-fashioned one even back then, manually operated by an elderly Negro named Herman, who I saw almost every day.

I said hello, stepped inside and exchanged the usual pleasantries. He turned the big crank from right to left to shut the door. When the gate was nearly closed, some-one called his name from the hall outside. Herman turned the crank backward, reopening the door. A secretary lady said, "Hey, Herman, would you mind dropping this off at the jail?" and gave him a big manila envelope.

Herman shut the doors again and turned to me. "Mr. Ed, you're going up to the jail. Would you give this to them?"

He went back to his controls, and the car rose. His back was to me, so I stole a peek inside. Inside was everything. The full report. Officers' names, badge numbers, past history, and testimony about the incident. Five seconds earlier or five seconds later and those elevator doors would have been closed, and I would have been out of the game.

When we got up to the jail, I thanked Herman for the ride, went into the men's toilet, barricaded myself in a stall and copied down everything in my notebook. When I was done, I gave the envelope to the jailer's assistant, wished him a jaunty good evening and returned to the paper to write the story. Mr. Clouse ordered page one replated and the story ran eight columns right under the nameplate. With my byline. The head was in 86-point Marathon Condensed: GANGSTER ELEMENT IN POLICE POINTS TO JOSEPH. Not exactly the best head, but the one Mr. Clouse liked. Readers had to get down into the story to find out that the poor black man was a numbers writer and that crooked cops were apparently trying to take over the entire racket to help Pete Sells start up his own policy book. No one in authority could be reached for comment at press time.

The next day the mayor called a press conference to denounce the publication of the article. He didn't deny the accuracy of anything except the headline, or claim that the facts had been taken out of context, but he said, with his customary artlessness, that he didn't know how "this kind of information got into the press of this city."

I never told my city editor how I got so lucky. He never asked, and from what I understand Mr. Clouse never asked him. From that day forward, however, my career was secure. It soared—while everything else in the city was going to hell in a Studebaker.

Cynthia McConnell:

Nobody can see me when I'm on the move this way, not always knowing where I am even after I've arrived. I fall back on other resources, which may be given to some of you one day if you're unlucky enough to be both angry and full of sorrow when you cross over. I see a wooden door with a painted sign *Défense d'ouvrir* and float right through it, as if being driven at high speed through a police roadblock without anyone seeing me—for no one can.

The rain is like a black theatre curtain that just keeps coming down and down and down without ever reaching the stage. The night is so dark that you can see only one block in either direction. The street lamps struggle to give aid though electric signs are the main source of light.

An enormous sign high up on one corner shows two boys playing football and flashes the message "Buckingham Cigarettes" and a strange motto: "Throat Easy."

I am on St. Catherine West. Automobiles suddenly emerge from nowhere as others turn and disappear forever. Men with upturned overcoat collars and water running off the brims of their sodden hats splash their way from one curb to the other. Women in furs and others in cloth coats huddle under their *parapluies* on the traffic island in the middle of the street. Many avoid the rain by loitering at the soda fountain and movie-magazine racks of a curiously named American Drug Store, which is staying open late tonight, as this is Saturday.

Some signs keep blinking, others never darken for a second. Canadian National Telegraphs. Sweet Caporal Cigarettes. Souvenirs. At long last a boxy tram lugs onto the scene clumsily, like a man heading home at three in the morning after a night on the town. It's the No. 41, returning from the East End night spots around the Main, the ones with "the highest calibre of Negro divertissement," and heading west to the uptown spots.

And yet just as I reach this place in time and space I'm just as quickly somewhere else.

Back in the city of my birth (and death), it's late spring, and Commerce Street on a warm day has never looked more like itself. Long rows of automobiles are parked grille-to-rear-bumper on both sides of the street. A thick crowd seems to move as a single mass of humanity although each person appears to be heading in a different direction. There are men, many of them bare-headed, in their shirt sleeves, with their neckties loosely knotted, and women in print dresses, some with reluctant children hanging on. Young people. Sale signs beckon from the shop windows. Big letters on marquees shout the names of the new motion pictures. A waiter or a bartender, for he could be either, with the hem of his white apron falling well below the knee, crosses into view. A bald man with a cigar in the corner of his mouth and his hands in his pockets stares up at the Tontine Building. When I lived here I never had much occasion to look at the tops of buildings, but now I see them in all their variety. At street level, most look essentially the same. Only the topmost floors have ornaments that make each one distinct. For the most part I suppose it is only spirits that take such pleasure in them from above. For instance, I never once thought of what was on the roof of Mrs. Schwartztruber's Fashions for Ladies when I shopped there and made sketches of new styles in my mind, but the view is fascinating. I can see the Mount Royal Club that Jim Joseph and Pete ran together before their partnership broke up. The No. 57 streetcar stops outside the Congress and a tangle of people tumbles out the doors—more people that you could think would fit inside, like a clown car at the circus. While the streetcar is stationary, a fellow hurries across the street diagonally. He's obviously heading for the railroad station. He has a straw hat and an ill-fitting light suit, a necktie so loud it screams, and white shoes. He carries a roll of material or papers under his left arm, and a pasteboard suitcase in his right hand. A real low-life, I imagine. He moves much faster than necessary, making himself conspicuous. I get the feeling he might have been a passing acquaintance of Pete's, and I'm never wrong when I get such feelings.

I can only look down on all of this razzmatazz and wish that I had lived some other life. One doesn't know such things until one is gone. What an astonishing surprise to discover that the spirit still grows after the body begins going in the opposite direction.

Edwin Staffel:

These events became a long, drawn-out melodrama, fascinating everybody around here from the Prohibition years to the Depression and far beyond. One easy explanation, back in the '30s, at least, was that the stories helped take people's minds off what they saw when they looked out through their kitchen windows. Sometimes clichés are true.

My own family wasn't badly off. My parents weren't Lebanese but Syrian. They changed the family name to Staffel, which they got from a luggage and leather-goods shop called Staffel & Spitznagel. I gave myself the name Ed, though my passport stills lists my first name as Sariyah, a common Arabic name for boys. It means "he who travels by night." It is supposed to be a compliment. My people, like all of the local Lebanese and Syrians, were Christians, but those of us born here were different from our parents; we didn't care to re-enact their lives but wanted to live our own. We went to movies and drank milkshakes and all the rest of it, and we chose the names we wanted to answer to. Go into a bar and shout "Hey, Ed," and I'm the first person to turn around.

The Depression was indeed depressing. Everything that was green not that long before suddenly turned brown instead. There were plant closings, layoffs, empty storefronts, hobos and bums, everything you've heard about. My father lost his job as a die-setter and tried to make up the loss, never with too much success, with handyman work. Mother got a part-time job at the bakery counter of the A&P on Chippewa Street, thanks, I suspect, to the store's assistant manager—I forget his name—who I've always assumed was sweet on her.

I came of age right in the middle of all this despair. Even while I was still at Bishop Dempsey High School, failing wood shop, to my father's dismay, but getting good grades in English, typewriting, and public speaking, I considered going out to California once I had finished my education. Instead I stumbled onto the only piece of luck anybody in our family was having in those years. Because I had my own bicycle, I was taken on at Western Union, filling in for the other delivery boys on holidays, sick days, and weekends. Odd hours, a few here, a few there, either before school or after school or even during school lunch break. One night I had to deliver a wire to Mr. Clouse at the *State Journal*. I saw him briefly standing in the newsroom—everybody in the city knew him by sight from all the photos of himself he published—but I didn't want to approach because he was bawling out a lad only a little bit younger than me. Firing him. I heard him yell, "You'll never be a copy boy anywhere again!" The fellow was trembling as he ran, almost stumbling, out of the office. I gave Mr. Clouse the envelope and waited to see if he wanted to dictate a reply, the way you're supposed to.

I don't know what possessed me. "Mr. Clouse," I said, "What's a copy boy do? He delivers pieces of paper. That's what I'm doing now. I'm good at it. I'm fast. You can ask anybody." My question must have sounded stupid, and it was. I naturally had an idea of what copy boys did from going to movies. They were young men and boys at whom other people, adults, were constantly shouting "copy!" But before I could convey my knowledge out loud, Clouse gave me a dour look (I didn't know then that this was his most common expression) and glanced over at one of the men sitting around the big horseshoe-shaped desk, running their pencils furiously over half-size sheets of cheap yellow copy-paper. He made a gesture—no, that's not right; he just put on a certain look that seemed to say "throw this kid out"—and turned on his heels and disappeared into a glass cubicle stacked high with all kinds of papers and obsolete copies of the *Congressional Record*. The man on the receiving end of Clouse's demand looked into my eyes for a moment. I don't know what he was thinking. "If you can start right this minute, I'll show you what to do," he told me. "This is unofficial, you understand. They'll hire some other kid tomorrow. But you'll get a little unpaid experience at least." Maybe he was recalling his own tyro days. I never found out, because he died of a heart attack not terribly long afterward, just as I was coming to know him a bit, or as much as someone just starting out can ever know a stranger even older than his own parents.

To make a long story as short as possible—something I literally learned to do when I later filled in for one of the men on the rim—I kept coming in night after night, ignoring orders to stop doing so. I was the quickest to respond when any of the reporters cried "boy!" or "copy!" waving something they were sending off to the desk. With my last pay packet from Western Union I bought a big tray of doughnuts and laid them on the half-broken-down table where some of the world's worst-tasting coffee was percolated. Once I did that, some of the men started talking to me. Mother, a smart woman, heard me tell the story, and managed, with what secrecy I don't know, to start bringing home stale boxes of what were called Mrs. Parker's Powdered Doughnuts, an A&P staple, which I laid out buffet-style every couple of days. When consumed with day-old coffee, they evidently didn't taste too bad.

Nobody stayed a copy boy for long. If you did, they figured you lacked the ambition or talent or brains to do anything else. When I graduated from high school in the spring of '37, I went looking for full-time permanent work, and determined to try the newspapers again. By then the *State Journal* had gobbled up the old *Inter-Ocean* without so much as good-bye or good riddance, and the

McConnell Trust, as the *State Journal* called it, bought the *Enterprise*, becoming the *Register-Enterprise*. (A sad use of a hyphen. The name plates were starting to look like tomb-stones. In conversation, most people went on referring to the *Register* as just the *Register*.)

There were too many newspapermen for the jobs that came open. That was on the one hand, you might say. On the other hand, it was clear to everyone that the De-pression, which had beaten us down and humiliated us, and saw a whole generation of children stunted, if not suffocated, in the thick, fog-like shadows of want and worry, was beginning to lift. After an unnatural absence, the crocuses seemed to be reaching for the sun again. Or, as Mr. Clouse would have put it, classifieds were up five to six per cent and national linage about the same or better, what with all the various vaguely worded remedies for ail-ments of interest to women in distress and men in despair.

Such were the conditions when I stumbled bravely into that city room, my hand still warm from the gradua-tion handshakes from the school principal and a member of the board of education. I have a snap my mother took of me on graduation day. Looking at it, I can only admire my ignorance of how I obviously must have seemed to adult men, sophisticated men, as I thought they must be. My shoes were all scuffed and my trousers were so short they showed far too much of the argyles in which I took such pride. American kids—real American kids—had cowlicks. I didn't, but I nonetheless followed the com-mon practice of all us slightly dark-complexioned males and slicked everything back.

I knew from others that Mr. Clouse did all the hiring. Nobody else had any real authority in staffing matters. Still looking, I suppose, like the acne-scarred delivery boy bringing a telegram (or a prescription from Walgreen's, etcetera), I penetrated about as far as Mr. Clouse's famous glass cubicle. For a short man he always maintained a commanding bearing, and I noted how he dressed: everything fitted him perfectly and made the whole far greater than the sum of the individual garments. Unlike early photos I would see of him later on, he had what was fashionable for the time I'm speaking of: a neat black moustache, like two thin elongated spear points. I realized that he was wearing some sort of cologne.

I introduced myself awkwardly, but fairly well nonetheless, for I knew what I was doing this time and explained that I'd do anything, absolutely anything, to get into the newspaper game for real. The fact that I had used far too much pomade on my hair and was sweating no doubt made me look even more nervous than I actually was. And no matter what I did to my shirt-tail, it refused to remain tucked. As it happened, the shirt is what saved me. As he listened, Mr. Clouse kept looking at it. It was my Sunday Mass shirt, cotton with an old-fashioned detachable collar. No doubt remembering his own first hunt for a job—when would that have been? 1905 or so?—he suggested, in a brusque, business-like way, that I return and see him next Monday or maybe Tuesday "around this time." In what sounded more like an order than a suggestion, he said I should always wear a white shirt—and a necktie too.

I went home and told Mother. She was proud of me, but concerned about the expense, though she didn't say so outright. "Now I'll be boiling the shirts we have to buy for you." Only later did her real concern come to the surface: "This city's run by the Americans," she said. "You know. American *gangsters*." The last word was a close to a whisper. I assured her with a light laugh that her boy would watch where he was walking.

Shortly afterward, the business about the shirt explained itself. I hadn't been at the paper long before I learned that sometime before my serendipitous arrival Mr. Clouse had had one of his temper spells and ordered the firing of yet another copy boy, one who assumed his poverty had given him the right to appear for work in a red striped jersey—in Mr. Clouse's words, like "some French youth for hire," so I was told. A year or two went by before I acquired a second pair of shoes but I always went everywhere in blindingly white shirts. And I set about learning the workings of the newspaper, which I imagined were pretty much the same as newspapers everywhere.

The men on the rim were already at their chairs when I arrived at work, a few days after being sent to the Medical Arts Building to get a clean bill of health and then to the teller's wicket in the lobby, next to the classifieds counter, to be signed on to the payroll. Yes, all the men wore white shirts but the deskmen at least worked in their shirt sleeves, wearing either sleeve garters or rubber sleeve cuffs to keep them from being stained with ink from the galleys. Their shoulders were rounded as they sat along the convex side of the desk in a big U-shaped formation. Opposite them, in the middle of the horseshoe, facing outwards, was the slot man, a serious-looking old gent who had worked his way up through every job in the editorial department to achieve this most important post. His name was Mr. Nithman. He had been an almost regal reporter until, it was said, his legs gave out. He had covered the Great Fire of 1905, and here and in other cities had reported on murder trials, suicides, judicial hangings, and every kind of political event or intrigue. He kept a bottle of rye whiskey in his desk drawer, along with his pica ruler and his picture-sizing wheel. Reporters working in the traffic jam of desks known as the coop would shout for one of the boys (there were three of us at the time) to take their finished stories and run—even when there was no great urgency—to put them in Mr. Nithman's wooden tray, from which Mr. Nithman would distribute among the deskmen, one for you and one for you and so on, as though he were dealing cards. The deskmen would mark them up in pencil, translate the writing into utilitarian English, shorten them, change them all around, and apply the copy-editing rules they all knew by heart because they weren't anywhere written down.

Woe betide him who disobeyed one of the rules. For instance, cigarettes always had to be called cigars, because Mr. Clouse believed cigarettes were leading today's youth down what he called, with unintended quaintness, the primrose path. The deskmen likewise would exercise great caution in letting the word *radio* slip into news stories, for radio was our rival. The rule was suspended, however, when we reluctantly began printing daily listings of the local stations, information the public demanded and I suppose depended upon. The program details were set in agate, the hardest-to-read size and font, which the compositors in the Back Shop called 6-point Gideon, but not in the presence of Mr. Clouse who, though not a regular churchgoer as far as anyone knew, considered the jest sacrilegious.

There was one reporter who still turned in his copy in flowing longhand, as though the world had not changed at all, as though typewriters were still rarities and there were no autos, no radio, of course no world war, and possibly only streetcars drawn by horses that pawed at the paving bricks and shook their horsey jowls from side to side like some blustering rotund cigar-chomping congressman committing an oration on the floor of the House. Everybody else typewrote, furiously, even when speed was not required, as though punishing the keys, and except the Society editor and the one or two other women in the city room, using only two fingers per hand. With a deadline pressing down, the reporters would shout "boy!" as they finished writing each take, a take being three or four paragraphs.

"How many takes you got to come?" Mr. Nithman might scream.

"Eight, looks like, maybe nine."

Mr. Nithman had such conversations without looking directly at his interlocutors. He communicated through a sour facial expression meant to show disdain for other people's incompetence or long-windedness. When the deskmen were done with the copy, Mr. Nithman recovered it with his seasoned grimace. He had big layout dummies spread around his side of the desk. The advertising department had already sketched in the ads in pencil. Working with the remaining space, he would find the right spot in loose accord with priorities established earlier, in the daily editorial meeting, and write an appropriate head and a series of subheads and decks. These had to fit to the letter and adhere to an entirely different set of arcane protocols that also never seemed to have been written down, some of them antiques of uncertain origin, others Clousean. Then, with a big swoosh, the pneumatic tube system suspended from the ceiling would blow the story inside a brass cylinder to the composing room, a clangy, stifling and Dickensian sort of place where the foreman, wearing luxurious whiskers like some ancient general, distributed the body of the stories to the men operating a bank of Linotype machines, though compositors, working at the stone, still set large heads by hand. Each page of type was locked into the heavy frame of its galley, then slid onto a waist-high dolly called a turtle or, more commonly, a truck (hence a coveted "double-truck ad" spread over two pages, as when the department stores were advertising big sales at Christmas and Easter, or crooked politicians were advertising themselves during election campaigns).

Photos and line art were made in the engraving department, upstairs, a dangerous place where men transferred an image to a metal plate of the right thickness which they then covered with a red powder called dragon's blood and dipped into a hideous bath of acid. The red stuff adhered to the image but let the acid eat away the rest, leaving what was in effect one big piece of type except with a picture instead of a letter or a word. The engravers were seldom spoken of, or to. Perhaps because working with acid was inherently hazardous, perhaps because they were foreign-speakers who worked out of sight of everybody else. There was something spooky and unpleasant about them, like gravediggers.

The wheels turned all day long. When the proofing room, where men read every word of the news aloud to one another, finished their work, and the ink-stained men in the back shop had completed their own tasks, in short when everything else that had to be done actually was, then, at precisely the same time every day, Mr. Clouse would enter the press room, where the printers wore brimless caps folded out of newsprint. He would nod in a certain way at the foreman, who would depress a red button the size of a marshmallow and the press would begin to rattle until the walls shimmied like your sister Kate. The press and the bundlers would spit out the latest edition at a head-spinning rate, just like in the movies. Heavy rectangular truckers and grubby urchin newsboys with cheap caps waited in the back alley by the loading bays. It was the news, goddammit, and much of it was true.

I liked the company of these older men. In time, I got to know a few things about them, nothing really personal or private, but the kind of information editors refer to as background. There was a fellow who played poker all night every payday until dawn brought him back to the city room, hung over and destitute of means. Another one wore sharkskin shoes; he was our aesthete and our fashion plate. A few carried walking sticks while others dressed almost like bums. Quite a number had been in the war. You could always tell them apart from the others. They drank as much as the rest but they didn't have a good time doing so.

Eventually I had a desk of my own and a roster of the lowliest editorial chores. On Fridays the paper still printed something called the livestock report, a carry-over from the days when farmers were more numerous than rounders in the area around the Seventh Ward Market. Somebody, I was never sure who he was, an auctioneer perhaps, would phone with the week's bid-and-ask figures for spring hogs and such. Quickly and in an accent that tested my concentration, he delivered endless lists of numbers. Despite my good typing (forty words a minute) I wonder how many times I got prices wrong. Once the thing was set in type, and some new copy boy came running with a smeary galley from the back shop, I had to proof it. I also called every day at the Congress, the Florence and the other leading hotels to see if anybody had checked in who, in the opinion of the sharp-eared staff, might prove good interview material. Finally, I got to cover meetings, not of council or even the school board, but of the water board, for example. This put me inside

City Hall. Once I was there, the experienced reporters treated me differently, even letting me have a drink with them at the First National on payday. That's where I first heard talk about Jim Joseph. I mean serious talk, not mere street gossip or fanciful tales.

Allan Ostermeyer:

The Carpenter was sitting in a banquette in one of his lesser clubs, where he preferred to hold morning meetings. It had been refitted with a smaller table than before so that he could get in and out more easily. The club hadn't opened for the day. It was just waking up. People were cleaning the carpet while others set the tables. One man silently polished the long bar. The Carpenter had already dealt with a succession of petitioners but had one more to listen to before he could ask Jim to join him. Jim waited patiently across the room, out of the way. His host could see him there and gave him a signal by raising his eyebrows as though to apologize for the long delay. The visitor in the booth seemed to be caught in the middle of some difficulty involving the Irish and the Greeks—of which he himself was neither—and needed the Carpenter to act as the mediator. He described his predicament in greatly unnecessary detail but finally shook the Carpenter's hand and rose to leave. He was almost bowing as he took a few steps backward before turning and heading for the door.

The Carpenter motioned to Jim and apologized for

making him wait. He nodded after the departing fellow. "*Il parle trop. Il pourrait parler jusqu'à faire descendre Jésus de la Croix.*"

They got down to business. Jim put a packet on the table, containing the Carpenter's fee for arranging for the Paddock to receive the wire from the people in Buffalo who had rented or more or less leased it from bigger fish elsewhere. The wire was actually received at the Roosevelt, then retransmitted the short distance to the Paddock, so that, in the event of a raid, it could be shut down temporarily in an instant in the one place without necessarily raising suspicions about the other. By controlling the wire, Jim controlled all the bookies' vital source of information. That is why God had given us the wire, this was its function in the world. Jim was also heavily invested in coin-operated devices. It was like the policy book: a second fortune in the form of nickels and dimes, pouring in every single day and night, grossing a million, or maybe millions plural, over the course of a year. Across three or four states, his machines sold candies in every movie house, dispensed cigarettes in every public gathering place and factory, and offered prophylactics in the men's room of every bar or dive—the joints that also feature his simple punchboards but also pinball machines (highly lucrative) and, most important of all, slots. The slots were real money makers because the size and frequency of their payouts could be altered at will by a few machinists he kept on retainer.

"So I have all these different companies, some of them

incorporated in different cities, each of them 'owned' by friends of mine. But lately, let me tell you, I've been running out of cousins."

The Carpenter chuckled.

"The damned slots are very hard to get. I scraped up a dozen to start with. I kept them down in my own district—you know, down in the Triangle—but the power boys in town raised a big ruckus. With Prohibition gone, I guess the churches, the do-gooders and the opposition papers were looking for something to crack down on. Some new sin. It became a campaign."

The Carpenter was a wise bird. "They don't like the way you make money." He was probably thinking we and not you. "They don't think you equal them. But when you make money, you scare them. They think you earn it too easy." He laughed at the absurdity that what he and his guest did was easy, and Jim laughed right along with him.

"Our mayor, the one we put in, isn't a strong man, if you know what I mean," Jim went on. "A lot of the aldermen are big-money lawyers and business guys who barely put up with him, and they won't do that for much longer. They've started to work hard at what they call cleaning up the town. For some reason, the slots really struck a nerve. Somehow—it makes no sense—the slots got mixed up with the party girls in people's minds. So I'm trying to get more slots from any source I can while trying hard to hold onto the ones I got. The police chief, Nolte, is our man, but he's under a lot of pressure too."

The Carpenter looked thoughtful, as though he were

about to speak—but didn't, not at first. When he began, he spoke slowly. "I have always liked the way you use the word soup. It makes me smile. But the soup to this bloke and that bloke—ça *va faire*! You are giving them something. You need to sell them something that they can sell back to you. Then you become partners and they are not your enemy."

Jim's visits to Montreal were worrisome, as he had no way of knowing, other than oral reports from Kasdan, what trouble crazy Pete was getting them into when he was, by default, temporarily in charge. Yet the trips always produced results. Jim had to contemplate the Carpenter's words until he emerged with their meaning, their message. He shored up Klein's authority as mayor by getting him to propose that the city clamp down on slots. Soon there were constant raids on Jim's two main establishments. The slots were sometimes confiscated overnight, though they were never destroyed, and the nominal owners of the Paddock and the Roosevelt were fined a hundred dollars for each machine plus six dollars in costs. A very similar arrangement was worked out with regard to the houses. As for the clubs, the day after each raid—"raid" hardly seems the right term, it was more like a Sunday visit—everything was back to normal. Over time, more and more slots popped up. Jim was amazed at how the Carpenter, who claimed to have limited influence in his own city, was nevertheless so thoroughly connected to places in the United States—a hold-over from the booze-smuggling days.

Jim was busy taking delivery of more and more

the room, shattering a large mirror. I was terrified. I had
no way to call for help short of opening the windows and
hollering for a policeman. Pete smacked me in the face and
I fell to the floor, not unconscious, but dazed and hurting.
When I gathered my wits and got the energy to rise, he
was gone. The door was wide open. Later I remembered
he kept threatening me as I lay on the carpet. "You can't
ditch me. I'll be back." Something like that. There was
more but I can't remember it now.

Edwin Staffel:

That long wall of slots at the Parthenon was Jim's break-
through all right. The thinking went something like this:
If these respectable people, these bluebloods and industrialists, millionaires many of them, were enjoying themselves with his machines, then Jim too was respectable,
sort of, by association. This was the delusion he needed to
reinvent his life in the manner of his friend up in Canada,
or perhaps in a way even more grand and ritzy.

The Paddock and the Roosevelt, the policy book, the
wire and all the rest were profitable enough to allow him
to move downtown and open the club and casino of his
dreams. It would be such a fancy place that simply to call
it the finest nightclub and restaurant between New York
and Chicago would not be doing it justice. It would be
unprecedented, no expense spared, and would attract the
high rollers and big bankrolls from all over the East—and

beyond, from the North. In their next meeting the Carpenter laughed loudly and agreeably when Jim told him the name: the Mount Royal Club. "Montreal is, what is the word, flattered to give its name to your child. But you know that there is already a Club Mount Royal, on Sherbrooke, a place for the big blokes on Saint-Jacques. It is very chic... *et plate à mort*! There's no one louche there and no French either. The French businessmen, they have their own, the Club Saint-Denys, just as quiet. I know you may need my help in spreading the reputation of your dream—and I will need my small commission." He was still smiling. "One day, when you are successful, I will not be too modest to take credit for giving you the name!"

Cynthia McConnell:

I'd thought of moving away or, if not that, at least moving to another part of the city, but I was too stunned and afraid. But not so afraid as I was about to become. One evening I saw Pete standing in the entrance way of a building directly across the street. He wasn't looking up at my window, he was looking down at his feet, but I knew he wasn't there by accident. I may not have known all of his automobiles by sight, and in any case he was always exchanging them for others or simply buying more, but I started to recognize some of the ones I remembered, always parked where he knew I would see them. One afternoon I came home to find the tip of a white envelope slipped partway under my door. I knew instinctively what it contained. Pete didn't write very clearly but I knew even before untangling his grammar that he was asking for reconciliation. My hands shaking, I thought long and hard about how to respond. It was humiliating to go talk to Father but that's what I felt I had to do. I thought that I might see Hedy while I was there and that she'd help me to feel better, but Father himself answered the bell—this was highly unusual—and we went into the den. I recounted what had happened, and what was still happening, but I deliberately used language that wasn't in the least dramatic. I could see how concerned he was for me but his tone wasn't paternal. "Damn it, I've warned Joseph to keep that crazy bastard on a short rope. I'll have to take the matter into my own hands." His tone wasn't especially angry but the words suggested violence. I was frightened all over again.

"What are you going to do?"

I didn't think he'd tell me. "Well, Joseph obviously isn't going to go up against his partner. He's not cut out for that. Or maybe he's scared of him too. First thing I'll do is get Nolte over here for a man-to-man. You're not to worry. I'll take care of everything."

Edwin Staffel:

Jim bought a five-storey building right downtown, a block away from the Congress. Bought it for cash—by which I mean actual banknotes, a small suitcase full (which naturally made Kasdan the accountant come down with a bad case of the jitters). The property had formerly been a minor but perfectly decent hotel called the Belgrave. On the ground floor, the lobby gave way to a reasonably large restaurant. The second floor was divided into two full-size banquet rooms. The upper floors were what were then called sleeping rooms, some small, some larger. The very top was comparatively tiny and might once have been the domain of a husband and wife who worked there for years as the handyman and housekeeper, respectively.

Jim was tearing out interior walls, putting an entirely new facade on the building right over top of the existing one, and essentially creating a lavish restaurant, nightclub and casino from scratch. He ordered a huge electric sign to be suspended above the canopy that would extend the entrance over most of the sidewalk.

Eight or ten different contractors worked on the project at any given time. Jim was careful to bring them in from different cities. A warehouse space had to be rented for the temporary storage of all the liquor, glassware, tableware, draperies, linens, uniforms, kitchen equipment, safes and, yes, gambling paraphernalia, until it could all be installed and the doors opened to the public in a swank event, probably on New Year's Eve, a mere ten months away. Jim wanted and got the best of everything. One entire day was taken up with ordering the custom-made ashtrays and what he considered the perfect shrimp boats from a glassworks that had been in business for a hundred and twenty-five years. Reviewing, revising and printing the menus took up a lot of time. He was so wrapped up in the project that Zelfa hardly saw him for more than an hour at a time, but the Mount Royal Club was moving right along on schedule, or nearly so, soaking up enormous sums of money along the way. Kasdan kept issuing warnings and Jim kept reassuring him that everything would be fine. Pete, however, wasn't so sure.

In a confrontation that had many versions, Sells told Joseph he wanted to dissolve the partnership and go his own way. "I've worked too hard for you to put my share of what we've made into all this," he said. "I don't know anything about running a joint like this—and neither do you." He said he'd be happy to take half of what cash remained, plus the Paddock and maybe the Roosevelt too, and chop up the policy book with him, taking half. Jim said the hard bargaining would have to wait but that they would work out something satisfactory if Pete would stay on through the grand opening. Pete agreed to hang on until then, though neither party was remotely happy.

It was at that point that I got the most important phone call of my life.

The young guy who was working the police beat (my old territory) called the city room to say that the cops had found a body in an apartment building on Marion Street and it was awful and he needed a photographer right away before the cops could throw him out. The kid's voice was crackling. I lit out right away, yelling at the photographer to follow me, and I'll never forget the scene. How could I. Those who lived nearby told the cops that they hadn't seen or heard Cynthia McConnell for days. One of them telephoned the police after she knocked on Cynthia's door but got no answer—other than a terrible smell.

When I first saw the body lying in the middle of the room I thought she was dressed in one of those fancy evening gowns made up of little glittery squares of foiled material all sewn together, sort of like chain mail. Bits of the dress appeared to be moving slightly. Getting closer I saw that the motion was caused by bugs crawling over the body in waves. Cynthia McConnell was on her back, as white as ivory, with one shoe on and the other off. Her hair covered the top part of her face. She'd been shot— only once, as far I could tell without getting any closer, but one of the cops was kneeling down looking for other wounds. The reporter who had phoned me left to go vomit in the toilet. The photographer arrived panting, and was right behind me. He held up his Speed Graphic to begin shooting but I stopped him. "The officers will take care of that," I said. "Get a shot of the front of the building." Chief Nolte arrived to take charge. He looked pale. I had no idea what would happen next.

You can imagine the uproar. The next morning's *State Journal* ran the banner SOCIETY MURDER! and the subhead "McConnell Heiress Found Shot to Death." The afternoon *Register* had a different interpretation. "Tragic Death of Prominent Young Woman" went the head. The deck added: "Mystery Surrounds Apparent Suicide." But of course there was no mystery, and no suicide. In the Final, the *Register* at least vouchsafed the following surmise: "Police Suspect Foul Play In McConnell Death."

When Nolte first broke the news to him, Cynthia's father recounted his daughter's fears and started to demand the arrest of Pete Sells, which in the circumstances seemed a logical enough first step. Pete was apprehended at Superior Billiards where he was running balls at a hundred bucks each. He was locked up on suspicion but at the bail hearing the next morning was freed on a $10,000 bond, which poor Kasdan was dispatched to pay in cash—small bills mostly, well used, with non-consecutive serial numbers, and an unusually large proportion of two-dollar bills. Such was the standard parimutuel bet, and our town has always been a two-dollar burg, though Jim's plan for his tony club and casino was intended to change that image of the place.

An elaborate melodrama began. In the most recent election, Karl Metzger had won a seat in Congress, another sign, many thought, that the Democrats were at least beginning to lose some of the ground they had gobbled up in 1932. But that didn't mean that he had abandoned his law practice. On the contrary. Over the howls of the mayor and the whole combination, he browbeat the state's attorney into putting the Sells matter before the spring grand jury—fifteen citizens whose names, addresses and occupations were then published in the newspapers, as per the curious custom at the time. In terms of the sides arguing for Pete's guilt or his innocence, there was much decidedly unorthodox activity. Many of us thought that the grand jury would fold like a road map, but it returned a true bill.

Locally at least, that's to say across the territory corresponding to Jim's little criminal empire, the proceedings were viewed as the sort of spectacle that had mesmerized the whole nation during the Leopold and Loeb case. Did Sells too think he was untouchable? Metzger and Clouse did everything but paint Pete with horns and cloven hooves. While Sells' demonization may not have been inaccurate, it was also true that there was no physical evidence tying him, or anyone else, to the crime. Pete furthermore had a valid alibi in the form of two street darlings and assorted bartenders, rounders, and gamblers. Suffice it to say that, in the backwater local version of the trial of the century, Sells, after two and a half weeks' agony in the courtroom, was found innocent. The Clouse crowd came pretty close to being cited for contempt when they hinted broadly that Jim's people had gotten to the judge, to which accusation one of the Josephites was heard to reply, "If he was a waiter, they'd call it a tip."

Poor Mrs. McConnell, who never was less than psychologically anemic, had a genuine breakdown, laid low, permanently, it was correctly feared, by the death of the daughter she had never seemed able to embrace the way she knew a mother should. Zelfa Nassif Joseph, hitherto a strong and generally silent woman, likewise went to pieces, knowing that her brother hadn't been in complete control of himself for some years and fearing that the verdict had been incorrect, though she told no one this, not even her husband, who nonetheless knew what she was thinking, for he was thinking much the same.

Not long after the acquittal, Pete demanded—demanded this time, not asked—that he be allowed to cash out so he could set up his own operation, but after some pleading by Jim he again agreed to remain until after the grand opening of the Mount Royal.

McConnell *père*, understandably enough, turned on both Joseph and Sells, thus putting himself in league somehow with Metzger. The world was coming apart.

Cynthia McConnell:

The funeral was said to be the biggest anyone could remember. I was the star attraction, looking serene and not at all waxy, as I had expected, but wearing a dress I certainly never would have picked out for myself. Poor Mother had to be helped slowly down the aisle by Father with the aid of Hedy, whose face looked to be almost melting with grief. Most of the pews were filled. All the family was there of course. My brother delivered a eulogy, revealing feelings I never even remotely suspected he had in him. Every city official and functionary was there. Chief Nolte wore his dress uniform with epaulettes and gold braiding. Girls I had gone to school with and their parents were there. So, it seemed, was everyone with whom Father had ever done any business, which is to say a great throng of people I'd never seen before. Those were the pews on the one side of the aisle. On the other side sat row after row after row of McConnell Steel workers, dressed in their best clothes, which were not always that good. Men held their flat caps in their laps and their wives clutched little bags. Handkerchiefs and hankies fluttered as people daubed at tearful eyes. Reporters sat erect in the back row, straining to hear over the echoes. The Episcopal priest was solemn to the highest degree. The music swelled and sobbed. I counted thirty-one cars full of mourners and their flowers following the hearse to Pig Iron's creepy mausoleum.

Everyone seemed to be on edge, but I was beyond all that.

Edwin Staffel:

I knew I was probably making a foolish move in leaving the *State Journal*. Mr. Clouse would never forget me much less forgive me. That's how he was. He hated even people he'd never met and didn't stop hating them even after they died, giving them an odd sort of immortality. I was still young enough that I might have become the editor in some year far away, but I couldn't resist Jim's offer to act as a sort of press agent—not the salary or the excitement.

In a remarkable feat of organization, costing an enormous pile of dough, Jim Joseph was actually going to have the Mount Royal's grand opening on time. He was anxious that the crowd on the big night not consist primarily of shuffle artists and left-handed characters who were heavy and puttin' on the dog. His exact words to me were: "This is not some hash joint I'm building here. We don't want mugs getting too gay with the flow." The Mount Royal Club was to be the ultimate fan-light operation.

The space was amazing. The lounge was made up of small round tables, not too close together but not far apart, forming a crescent around the big stage inside another half-circle, big enough for a chorus line. There would be first-rate acts, Jim explained, and one of my jobs would be to book them and pamper them and handle the publicity, and put Crisco on the griddle when necessary. As for the casino, a one-flight hoof upstairs, it was resplendent, with carpets your feet could get lost in and felted walls with velvet trim and a cut-glass bar from Italy. All-new facilities for every game of chance you could imagine had been hand crafted. There were fifteen-hundred-dollar roulette wheels, lavish dice tables, and barboot, keno, skin games—all the fast games—and yet some that were meant for slow show. The man in Montreal had sent down a French guy he knew who could be on the stick at the wheel and also run twenty-one.

I didn't understand what the deal was, but I knew that Montreal was selling us a vastly bigger service as well. Montreal knew all the deep players from New York, Philadelphia, Baltimore and so on, and was being paid, a lot, I would imagine, to invite them. I kept wondering whether the Carpenter himself would show up, but I didn't ask. That wouldn't have been polite. I'd just graduated from my modest background and I didn't want to stub my toes. I was securing three floors of the Congress Hotel, finding hostesses to meet various trains, and just generally making arrangements. Another of my jobs, and maybe the main reason Jim hired me, was to massage my typewriter.

Jim wanted me to write a show biz column for the papers. I gathered that it should be something like Ed Sullivan's "Little Old New York," but a small-time version. Small time was the biggest time we had, though Jim's idea was to change that. He wanted me to ballyhoo the Mount Royal, the acts we were bringing, the food, the wines, and the relaxing games. I gathered that if I felt the urge to take the odd potshot at the scissorbills and moralizers that would be all right (so long as he saw it first—"I don't like surprises"). This put me in a tight spot right from the beginning. Suspecting what the reaction might be, for I heard the talk all over town—everybody did—I nevertheless approached the editor of the *Register* to see about buying space. He practically exploded.

"You must be out of your mind. Your new boss and my boss are at each other's throats. Jesus Christ, Mr. Mc-Connell wanted to have Sells electrocuted! His temper had to be restrained. He's convinced that your boss's partner killed his daughter for God's sake, and frankly so do I. So does everybody. Get out of my sight before I call some heavies in the circulation department to throw you out bodily." He meant the goons who drove the delivery trucks. "Go back to your sewer."

That certainly hadn't gone well, so I tried to reason out how I might approach Mr. Clouse. After all, he knew my work, and had come to trust me, I think, as much as he did anyone, though this wasn't saying much. If I avoided the potshots, I might be able to negotiate with him, for I knew his weakness: greed. I decided to try making a deal, though I had no authority to do so. In the end, I managed to buy a regular spot on the Amusements page every Monday, when the paper was at its thinnest. The space was two columns wide and six inches deep including the standing head. The arrangement included two stipulations. One was that the paper wouldn't print "Advertisement" over the piece, as was normal policy in cases where an ad was made up to fool the naive into mistaking it for legitimate editorial matter. The other was that I would pay for the space personally rather than go through Kasdan (who would reimburse me). I guess I always thought that Mr. Clouse was a crook, if only in small ways, nickel-and-diming his partners.

I began right away puffing up the pending opening of the city's "swank new nitery." I wrote about its looks ("streamlined in the vogue of today"), about all the celebrities and upper-crust types who could hardly wait to get in, about the first-class menu, and about the top-of-the-line entertainment, from famous crooners to "fast-action swing bands" imported at great expense (which was actually true). As for gambling, that was implied in the boast that the Mount Royal Club would offer "the finest personal entertainment facilities anywhere between New York and Chicago." Stealing an idea from *The Rider* of Mr. Clouse's youth, I filled up the bottom with corny jokes, plus a few tips of the hat to local dignitaries.

My biggest success, one that made Jim take an additional liking to me, came when I got the major radio station in town to agree to broadcast the first-night festivities from the lounge, though at one point the deal almost fell apart until Jim took the musicians' union aside and had a word with them. For a while I thought I had the same magic touch as those publicity men at the Hollywood studios. But as I was laying on the superlatives with a trowel and Montreal was spreading word throughout the secret world of the high rollers, the actual launch seemed to be coming apart.

The talk around town, which I believed to be accurate, was that Zelfa Joseph, distraught over her brother's role in the death of the McConnell girl, blamed her husband for the tragedy. The crime itself, combined with the lurid trial, had brought disgrace on her parents, who commanded her to separate from her husband and return to the family nest. Several of the congregation seemed to shun the Josephs when they attended Mass at Our Lady. As for Jim, he was in a bad frame of mind and moved out of the apartment, I presume because it reeked of sad memories. He took up residence in his office in the Mount Royal, sleeping on a roll-away bed amid stacks of invoices and building materials, for the whole structure seemed to have become full of these items in the frantic run-up to the grand opening.

Jim had made Pete promise to stick around for that majestic event, after which they would split, even-steven. Sure enough, Pete turned up every few days and got in the way. The temperature always seemed to change the second he entered the place. The workmen and the staff and the hangers-on and city inspectors and the like would turn their volume down to a collective whisper and make a special effort to keep their eyes on whatever it was they were doing. To make matters worse, McConnell had obviously sworn vengeance against the whole enterprise and was doing whatever he could to bring us tumbling down. The *Register*'s man in the capital reported gleefully that a bill would be introduced in the forthcoming session of the legislature to make operating a numbers book a felony. Hearsay, nothing concrete but very worrisome nonetheless, held that Metzger was in conference with the federal tax authorities, convincing them to take action against Jim. The sputtering fuses on people's tempers were growing mighty short. I wasn't there to hear it, but the others gave me the lowdown on a heated, almost violent argument between Jim and Pete, though nobody I talked to could tell me what had provoked it or exactly what was said, such being the thickness of the walls and the constant commotion in the place. All they could tell me was that it certainly didn't sound good. Sounded like big trouble in fact. I considered waiting for a relatively calm moment to bring up the subject with Jim, but there were no quiet moments anymore. Then, all of a sudden, Jim left town for a few days. Montreal, I guessed.

Allan Ostermeyer:

In the end it all came down to this: a reduction, as a French chef might say, a reduction of experience, horror, shame and fear, all stirred around and blended into one. Jim Joseph had told Charpentier the entire story from first to finish. In their profession—whatever you choose to call it, whatever it may actually be—plain-spokenness is respected all the more because it's dangerous enough to be rare. Once he had explained the problem, Jim asked the Carpenter for his help in solving it. Or rather, for making it go away.

The Canadian acknowledged what he was hearing but in such a way as to postpone his response: he'd have to think about it. Then—the story becomes stranger and stranger, or at least perplexingly anticlimactic—he invited his visitor to a hockey game.

It was December 12th of 1936. The two Montreal teams, the Maroons and the Canadiens, were playing at the Forum. The Carpenter's driver nudged his way through the thick traffic like a border collie in a flock of sheep. The whole way to Atwater and St. Catherine Street West the touring car schemed through the nighttime metropolis as the Carpenter entertained his guest with the information he would need for full enjoyment of the game, the first and almost certainly the only one Jim ever witnessed.

"This evening will be interesting because the blood between them is bad. They are full of *rancœur*. It is what the men that write about sports call a grudge match?"

Jim nodded.

"Last spring," the Carpenter continued, "the Maroons played against the Red Wings here. You should have been a witness to that. Six overtime periods! It ended at two-thirty the next morning when a player from Detroit called Bruneteau—'Mud' Bruneteau—finally broke the tie. The longest game in the history of hockey."

"Is this game tonight a French-English thing?"

"Yes and no. Most French, especially from the East End, they cheer for the Canadiens. You'll see in a minute that the jerseys are the red, white and blue. Not your red, white and blue from where you're from; the red, white and blue of the *tricolore* of France. People from West-mount and the other English areas, they yell for the Maroons who wear the purple. Most of the players on the Maroons are English. The most famous one, Conacher, comes from Toronto. He wears number three. A great big fellow, but getting too old to play soon. Used to be a football player. A baseball player too. Before the Maroons he played hockey in New York. 'The Americans.' You know the team, yes? It was owned by a bootlegger, or let's say a *contrebandier*, as the other word is getting old and worthless, like us, my friend, or like me at least. I have heard it said that this fellow I'm speaking about had partners who later died—but not for that reason. Legs Diamond and Dutch Shultz." He chuckled, as though satisfied that he perhaps knew a bit more than he was letting on.

"The Depression has been hard on the teams but more on the Maroons. But it is hard on all of us, am I right? The team is owned by two wealthy men, English, so the Canadiens are owned by two French. The four of them together own the Forum also. So you see how well we all get along when we make money together." The smile returned. He was having a good time.

The ticket-taker recognized the Carpenter and kept his eyes focused on his little counter top as the great man breezed by without hindrance with his visitor in tow. For Jim, the Forum, like most everything in Montreal, was a revelation. For one thing, it was enormous. The arena was also in a state of chaos that everybody involved seemed to take for granted even before the game had begun. Much later Jim learned that the building had nine and a half thousand seats. That night all of them were filled: the ones nearest the ice by the fat cats and their ladies, those farther up by the hoi polloi. Some of the former wore toppers while their wives or sweethearts were wrapped up like expensive gifts, but in furs instead of fancy paper. For their part, the riff-raff were an undulating sea of cloth caps, mostly, bobbing for a better view of the action about to commence. Between and beyond the seats were thousands of fans who would watch the game standing up the whole time. Many had smuggled themselves onto the premises. And many of these, and evidently many of the others as well, had brought liquor with them: the businessmen with their silver flasks, the workers with bulbous paper sacks. The Carpenter pointed across the great expanse to a high chain-link fence that separated the social classes. "It used to be that some would excite themselves and throw a bottle of Schenley at one of the players. Or at one of the bankers." He laughed.

It was no surprise that the Carpenter would command the best view of the ice that anybody could possibly secure. He panted as he took Jim on a long climb all the way up to the press box. The newspaper reporters either nodded politely or nervously and offered semi-formal welcomes to the Carpenter, as though they were afraid not to. The box was small and crowded but two more chairs were found. Next to the press box was what was called the fan-room. There, behind sound-proof glass, two radio announcers would report the game, one in English, the other in French, for their respective stations, one of them with the beginning phrase "General Motors Hockey Broadcast!" and the other "La Radio-Hockey General Motors!" Now everyone was waiting for the loudspeaker to address the multitude: "Ladies and gentlemen, *mesdames et messieurs*, would you please rise for our national anthem. *Mesdames et messieurs*, ladies and gentlemen, *veuillez s'il vous plaît vous lever pour notre hymne national*."

The Carpenter enjoyed being a host. "Let me tell you things to watch. You see the fellow in the suit way down there walking back and forth like a wooden duck in a shooting gallery? That's Cecil Hart. He is Canada's greatest coach. With him, the Canadiens won the Stanley Cup three times. Then the owners, they were stupid, they fired him. I know these men personally. They own the Blue Bonnets Raceway out on Décarie Boulevard where I sometimes have business. The story about them was..." He interrupted himself. "I don't know if this is true, but word was they did not want to have a Jew as head coach. Later the bosses of the team changed and the new owners asked him back again. He said yes if they hired Howie Morenz, number seven. He's the most popular player in Montreal. You'll see him down there. And watch for Jean Gagnon, they call him Black Cat, and Aurèle Joliat. Both of them very little fellows, skinny, but you can tell them apart without trouble because Aurèle always wears a little black cap on the ice—for good luck, you see. I'll point you to Toe Blake—that's his name, T-O-E—and Babe Siebert, the captain. He was traded but he's back this year. Poor man. His wife Bernice, she had a heart attack when giving birth and can't use her legs. Babe carries her in his arms to her seat every game. It is for sure a sad thing to see." He was about to go on when the puck was dropped and the uproar took over.

After the game, once enough of the crowd had funnelled out the exits, the two men left the press box. As they were approaching ground level, the Carpenter stopped. The pair of them were standing in a spot where departing fans had created a bare patch, though the noise of the crowd was still so deafening that they had to whisper hoarsely into each other's ear. No one could possibly overhear them. The frivolity was over, both in fact and in the Carpenter's voice.

"There's a man in this country that does the kind of job you were asking me about, or has done it in the past and maybe will do again, I don't know. He does not do it here, but only in other places. You would never know to look at his picture—I have only ever seen his picture—what his talent is. He is a very unusual man and he wants a great deal of money, or did in the past, ten or twelve years ago, when I learned of him. You understand this?"

"I understand," Jim said, hoping that he did.

"I was told once by someone I used to know that the people who would come looking for this man afterward—big bootleggers, you know, and the policemen—they would always search in the wrong country because the way he operated his profession was known only in a few places. Chicago. New York. You get what I'm saying?"

"Yes."

"He uses—if he is still alive and still in the business—uses a *mitrailleuse*." Jim must have looked puzzled. "They call what he has a *machine à* écrire."

The word "machine" somehow translated the term in Jim's brain. He shivered visibly. "If you can locate this, ah, individual, when could he do the job? How does he get paid?"

Joseph had other questions but the Carpenter cut him off. "Someone will contact you one day, maybe soon, maybe later, but perhaps not so much later. He will give you a message about the money. And, how would you say it, an agent would make sure that the man gets his pay, minus a commission. You would know that the job is done when you see it written in the papers."

Jim couldn't get to sleep that night, thinking about the newspapers and everything else. In the middle of his middle-of-the-night crisis of the soul he suddenly remembered the press box. I'll never be able to talk French myself, he thought. I can understand how you could teach yourself to speak French, even to write in French. But writing French on a typewriter, and fast the way those guys do, it's almost beyond my power to believe what I saw with my own eyes was true.

Edwin Staffel:

My teeth were chattering with excitement when I woke up that morning and practically ran down to the Mount Royal. You never saw so much commotion. The orchestra was rehearsing, polishers were polishing, carpenters were tapping in last-minute nails, table men were combing the baize. Bowls of cut-up onions were scattered everywhere, to soak up the new-paint smell. Downstairs everything was being scrubbed clean, even the stoves and iceboxes in the kitchen though they were so new they'd yet to be used. Upstairs, mechanics were doing things to the insides of the slots. I made my report to Jim about who had already arrived in town. He seemed distracted but said to me, "We should have chartered a train." I couldn't tell if this was a wisecrack. Stacked up on his desk were a hundred brand-new decks of Bicycles, for bettors often demanded a fresh one be unsealed when a game was waxing hot.

Darkness fell early as it does that time of year and as soon as it did Jim went from floor to floor telling everyone to get ready. The staff scattered. Women fixed themselves and wiggled into their uniforms, or all of them except the one female croupier (a new idea) who emerged in a red gown. Pete turned up on the second floor a short time later, already in evening clothes and looking angry or crazy, maybe both. He and Jim nodded across the room but didn't speak. The evening was going to be interesting.

The dining lounge and the downstairs bar started to fill up first. Jim played the role of host supremely well. The room was soon chock-a-block with local citizens, whether Parthenon members or minor professionals, some with their wives, out for a toot on the town. Each received a complimentary smile, a handshake and a few friendly words and best wishes for the holiday. Only minor things went wrong. The coat-check girl, who looked likely to end up with a little bankroll of tips by night's end, ran out of hangers and I had to dispatch a kid to the Congress Hotel for as many as he could carry. At one point, Pete went into the men's room and was washing his hands when one of the floor men entered. The men all wore tuxedos—special ones, without pockets, for you don't want pockets in a gambling den, however swanky. The fellow was hanging up his jacket prior to entering a cubicle, revealing the piece he was carrying in a shoulder rig. Pete suddenly spun him around and socked him in the jaw, sending him sprawling. "Who the hell hired a dub like you? A brown holster with a tuxedo! Jesus Christ! Where did you learn that? You're fired. Get out before I throw you into the street."

As the evening really got underway, the place became jam-packed, everyone dressed to the nines and excited. The city had never seen this sort of social event. Another hour or two and the big boys started to flow in. In contrast to the locals, they looked serious rather than excited. There were people from Buffalo, from Detroit, from Miami, people from who knows where. Persons of means, some of them accompanied by guys who didn't dare take a drink that night: the bodyguards. Since only verbal invitations had been sent out, no printed cards, it was inevitable that a few strange characters would slip in between the cracks. Jim was still glad-handing normal individuals when a highly excitable red-haired fellow in a bad suit rushed up to him and yanked his hand. "Jim, Jim. Great to see you again." Jim looked blank. "You remember me," the man insisted. "I'm Red, remember? Red. Red Stick. Red Stick from Baton Rouge." Jim shook his hand and moved away as Nolte, hired for the occasion and looking exactly like a cop in a penguin suit, slid into view and distracted the interloper with friendly chit-chat. Upstairs, money was flying around like it was a ticker-tape parade. The dice were hot, the cards were hot, the wheels hardly seemed to slow down for even a second. I actually saw one gentleman lay down forty thousand in one smack, not even blinking when he lost it. Kasdan and his under-lings were busy as beavers behind a fancy wrought iron cage and wore rubber thimbles on their counting fingers. Yet the jelly is one of the things I remember most clearly when I think back on the early part of that evening. For once, maybe for the only time, everybody got along, even when standing at opposite ends of the table during the heat of play. For that one slice of time, Greeks got along with Polacks, Turks got along with Frenchies, hunkies got along with boyos as Irish as Paddy's pig.

Cynthia McConnell:

I was there too, the lone representative of the McCon-nell clan. I saw everything that took place and heard every word that was spoken. Pete had taken yet another new girlfriend. She wore a slinky dress and a bruise over her left eye, for someone had "put a shandy on her glimmer" as Pete, who was fond of James Cagney movies, no doubt would have said. Pete kept calling her his lucky rabbit's foot. What a jackass.

In addition to a new girl, Pete had a brand-new auto-mobile, yet another one, an immense thing, powerful and garish, called a sixteen-cylinder Rockwell. He liked speak-ing about his automobiles as though they were women, and vice versa. He was known to refer to his new lady's bust as her grille. What on Earth had I ever see in him?

Long after midnight, when the paper horns had hooted

their last, the funny hats had been discarded, and the orchestra's jazz rendition of Auld Lang Syne had faded from memory, Pete and Jim Joseph had a terrifying argument in the office high up atop the Mount Royal. My ears perked up when the conversation turned to me, or the memory of me. Jim said Pete was getting crazier by the day and desperately needed help before he "killed somebody else." Pete blew up, calling Jim a liar, a weakling, a four-flusher, a cheapskate, and two or three other terms I don't care to repeat. Jim looked at the clock. "This party's probably going to go till daybreak or until whenever the last drunk goes home. It's late. You were done here hours ago. The time for you to go is now. We're through."

Pete reminded Jim that half the money was his.

"You'll get it all right, but you'll never understand it. It's not an end in itself, but it is how people try to get you."

"Get me! That's a laugh."

"The tax people aren't going to forget about you. You think they will if you tell them what they want to hear. But you're wrong. Trust me, you're looking at more courthouse time, and you won't walk out a free man on this one."

"You're talkin' about yesterday's laundry." Pete dismissed Jim with a snort and stalked out of the office.

Allan Ostermeyer:

Almost everybody heard the shooting, but Nolte and his men could find only two people who actually saw what happened. Two, that is, in addition to the passenger, who had gone into hysterics and was heavily sedated in Passavant Hospital (and would say nothing about it after coming around—and left town shortly thereafter, leaving no trace). A Miss Burkharter who lived in an apartment immediately across the street was looking out her window by chance when she saw the fancy auto pull up to the opposite curb. She saw the driver get out and walk around the front of the car to open the door on the other side, evidently for a passenger. This seemed odd. No one had ever seen Pete be gallant. As he was reaching for the handle, Miss Burkharter told the authorities, she saw a man emerge from a car parked two car-lengths behind and let loose with a Tommy gun. "Just like a motion picture," was the way she put it. She couldn't describe him. But a man named Schwanenbergh, urinating in an alley, glanced up when the shots began. He described the killer looking at the body for a few seconds after the firing stopped. He said something Schwanenbergh couldn't quite make out. He thought the assassin had a foreign accent though he wasn't positive. He was dead certain that the man was of average height and average physique, wore a dark hat and a dark overcoat, and drove away in a dark sedan. Three days later the police discovered a car they thought might have been what the *Register* kept calling the "murder car."

It contained no readable fingerprints, in fact no evidence of any kind, and had been reported stolen a week earlier.

Edwin Staffel:

About this turning point, I admit I know nothing more than what everybody who reads the papers came to know, which was not much. Many people whispered that McConnell had hired the Tommygun man to avenge his daughter's killing, but no hint of such opinion ever saw print. The case remained unsolved until history itself rendered it worthless to remember, except as a long-winded tale of what happened back in the old days, long ago.

Cynthia McConnell:

The tragedy of my murder is that I will never grow older than I was the instant that bullet tore into my left breast. My situation, however, has compensating advantages. I can travel at will without actually moving (it requires no effort whatsoever), can go backward and forward in time, can move about as easily as smoke leaves a chimney.

One day when, out of curiosity, I was spinning backwards, I rewound the film of the past, you might say, to the day following Pete's death, and fluttered my way into the morgue in the sub-basement of Passavant Hospital. There he was all right, lying on a white enamelled table that rested on cast iron legs. A big screw on one of the legs had been turned so that the end where his head was, cradled in a kind of steel pillow, was higher than his feet. His head was facing away from the wall, the eyes closed and his hair an uncombed mess. He was naked and understandably pale and he looked very tall, stretched out that way. Light shone down on him from the electric fixtures in the ceiling but he emitted no light in return. His thick chest hair was matted down and so was what grew down below. His sexual organ, which I confess I remember well, had flopped over to one side before rigor set in. Bullets had made ugly round holes in his upper body, in an almost straight line from below his right collarbone down to his left hip bone.

All four walls were white tile. There was a basin and three sinks. The spigot on one of them dripped loudly. As I vanished I was thinking that his life had been of almost no real importance whatever in the world. Soon I came to see that his death would have a different effect.

Edwin Staffel:

For better or for worse (much worse), the caking of Peter Sells was a dividing line. The good news was that once he was dead, other people ceased being shot in the streets quite so often. The Great War had let loose a new kind of violence everywhere; Pete's trial and death put the brakes on this pattern, at least in our little corner of the map.

But then everything that he and Jim had worked so

hard to create started falling apart fast.

Everybody knew that Pete murdered the McConnell girl but there was disagreement as to why. The cops rummaged around for a motive to help the prosecution, believing, as cops always do, that people who've been accused are obviously guilty or why would they be charged. They gathered evidence showing that the heiress to the McConnell fortune had broken up with Pete Sells, or he with her, or that she was stepping out on him or was thrown over for some other skirt, or many of them, and so picked a jealous argument. There was also the suggestion that he shot her because she knew too much about his business and would turn state's evidence. Any of these might have been true—or all of them. Many of those who liked to guess at Pete's motive said it was simply a matter of Pete being Pete, no more, no less. Guys who'd been to school with him knew he'd always been violent, even as a kid. Some brilliant minds thought he got used to killing the Hun in the war and liked it so much that when the war was over he lit out in search for substitutes. That's what people were saying. They were saying he was addicted to it, just as he probably was addicted to other stuff as well.

In the elections in '38, Representative Metzger, who, it hardly needs to be said, had most of the big local money behind him, knocked the incumbent Democrat out of his seat in the US Senate. Let me tell you, this was no easy feat in the Roosevelt years, but he was aided by an unfortunate scandal involving his opponent, a subject about which the public was kept highly informed, daily and Sunday, by

the *State Journal* and—this was a shock to almost everyone—by the *Register* as well. McConnell was changing
his political affiliations to give Jim some serious swatting.
Some were speculating that Jim soon might disappear,
perhaps of his own volition, or perhaps not. In any case,
there was no need for McConnell to take revenge on Jim
that way, for his life was crumbling anyway, all by itself.

Zelfa sought help from her priest. As she could not di-
vorce her husband and still receive Communion, she eventually decided, after much wringing of hands and saying of
the rosary, to separate from Jim. Jim, though perhaps not
surprised, was certainly crushed. That much was obvious
even at a distance: his gait slowed and stubble appeared on
his chin where none had been allowed before. The final
blow—at least it seemed final at the time—was Zelfa's an-
nouncement that she would leave the country, returning
to Beirut with her grieving mother and father. Pulling up
stakes, erasing the life they had always wanted and had
been proud of having made for themselves. Hearing this,
I thought to myself what I supposed others were thinking as well, but no one said out loud, leastwise not in my
hearing: now, with all of Pete's money, Zelfa and her parents would live like kings and queens in the Old Country.

These events reminded me of those passages in the Bi-
ble wherein Abraham begets Isaac who begets Jacob and
so on. As a US senator, Metzger had more power than his
former fellow congressmen could imagine—more power
not only federally but also, indirectly, at the statehouse.
He was quietly instrumental, but fiercely so, in getting

the Legislature to pass into law a bill that made operation of the numbers racket a felony. There was no question who this was aimed at, and Jim had to shut down the whole business before the measure took effect. This was a financial blow equal in its gravity to the personal blow of Zelfa's departure. Sure, he still had the horse wire and other things going on, but this legal development left a crater in his income.

At about this same time, a new mayor turned on Jim. Nolte was out as police chief, and the cops, accustomed to exacting modest fines when they discovered slot machines, began using sledgehammers and fire axes to smash them to smithereens, along with the premises in which they resided. For a little while, the machines in the Parthenon Club's billiard room were spared, locked up in their fancy wooden consoles, but eventually they simply disappeared, no one knew where. Hundreds of thousands of dollars were being drained from Kasdan's ledgers. Jim was determined to hold on to the Mount Royal, but he had to shutter the Roosevelt. As for the Paddock, it remained a profitable business but it wasn't any cash cow, and it was difficult to say what might happen to it in the longer term.

The blows kept raining down on Jim from the papers and the pulpits. Friends, customers and even mere acquaintances dropped away. How he must have longed for the days when he controlled the policy book and peppered the town with slots that could be set to pay out a penny on the dollar or whatever percentage he liked.

On some of his less-bad days, he put whatever energy he could muster into building up the coin-machine business. This was the opposite of what bootlegging had been, because he had no control over the candies and cigarettes being sold; he had to buy wholesale and sell retail, just like everybody else. One or two others with the same general background as himself, but minor people, amateurs, had also taken to this pursuit now that Pete wasn't around to scare them off. Once or twice some person or persons unknown would threaten the owner of one of the downtown movie houses if he didn't change the outfit from whose machines jujubes and Necco Wafers tumbled out with each five-cent pull of the lever. Once or twice there were even half-hearted tries at blowing the front out of a warehouse where pinball or midway claw-machines were stored and repaired. The numbers had been nickel-and-dime stuff, too, but Jim was one of the genius business executives who made a fortune from it. What he was doing was embarrassing.

He didn't drink any more than usual but he did get awfully itchy with the need to gamble. When somebody who doesn't feel lucky tries to gamble, he keeps trying and keeps losing. Jim needed more income and tried to organize the madams in the Triangle to form something like a madams' union with himself as business manager—something he never would have done when Zelfa was still in his life. It worked to some extent, but only some, for he didn't have the pull at City Hall any more. He was getting sick in the soul. He decided to offer Kasdan a half interest in the Mount Royal and the coin machine business with no immediate buy-in while he went back up to Montreal to see if times were still as good there as they used to be.

By then World War II had started. England at war meant Canada was at war as well. For a man of business, especially perhaps for one in decline, a war might spell opportunity. Then again, it might mean the opposite. He had to let me go, but he promised to send for me if things worked out.

Cynthia McConnell:

You people down below believe either that we are ghosts who haunt the living, begging you to let us breathe and be whole again, or else spirits who punish you for bad things you have done. I regret no longer being sentient and animate yet have no desire whatsoever to go through all that rigamarole again—all that emotion, growth, idleness, and pain. I'm neither a spook nor anybody's guardian angel. Not an avenging angel either; I have no wish to inflict revenge, certainly not on Pete even if that muttonhead were still alive. Nonetheless, once I began hovering around Canada I both felt and knew that I was in a much different place than I had been earlier.

Montreal was a city of big stone buildings: cathedrals, churches, convents, nunneries and monasteries, parochial schools, and Catholic hospitals; they were everywhere. And I thought I had grown up in city where everyone else was Catholic! But the city was made of other kinds of buildings as well, more vibrant, from great basilicas of commerce all the way down to the modest parish churches of day-to-day business, all crowded together at the shoulders, like passengers on a morning trolley. The Depression had obviously knocked the city on its knees, but not all of it, not the farther west you looked. And now there was a war on in Europe and Canada was a part of it. Young men were on the prowl for young women with whom to dance and laugh away their fears about the brevity of life. And there were older men—how could I not be reminded of Pig Iron McConnell—calculating the ways war could make them a first fortune, or another one.

I saw Jim Joseph in an overcoat and maroon scarf and wearing a new hat. He was striding diagonally across Dominion Square, a place surrounded on all four sides by tall office buildings. He stopped in the middle, not far from one of the statues and monuments, and peered at a small octagonal building hung with awnings. It looked like some kind of ramada, or a kiosk where you might purchase a train ticket. As he entered, another man was coming out, adjusting his clothing. When Mother would take me to Paris when I was an adolescent the others girls and I would giggle at the *vespasiennes*, those cast-iron structures that served such an important purpose for males of the species. In wintertime, Montreal might be too cold some days to relieve oneself. This was one of the little strategically placed pissoirs. Before I was too long in Montreal I learned here they were called *camilliennes*, after the mayor,

Camillien Houde, an energetic man with an enormous head who had done much to ease unemployment and poverty during the economic emergency, putting people to work on building projects and even turning his house in St. Hubert Street into a refuge for the poor.

Edwin Staffel:

The days passed by quickly and the nights had no flies on them either. After the Japs bombed Pearl Harbor, the city changed in a hundred ways all at once. Every mill, plant and foundry was suddenly going full steam ahead and the air grew dirty again, just as it had been in the twenties, and people were happy and nervous. The people got patriotic the same way they got religion.

With so many guys wanting to go off to war, there was a line of volunteers every day that ran from inside the main post office around the block past Walgreen's all the way to the Tontine Building. You would have expected the population to shrink, but just the opposite was true. The old burg was so flooded with people you could hardly find a furnished room. Groups of strangers shared tiny apartments. In some cases, three guys working at McConnell's, each of them on a different shift, would rent a room that had only one bed plus a sofa. Whenever the whistle was about to blow signalling the shift change, one of them would get up and run off to work while the one coming home would climb under the rumpled sheets. The same with stores and offices. Bookies in particular had trouble finding landlords. One bookie joint was in the backroom of a candy store on Commerce Street, the kind with a display of Whitman's Samplers in the front window. Another, on an upper floor of the Amber Building, used a milliner's shop as a front. Some mug in a hand-painted tie and a big boxy suit would suddenly appear in the little reception room where samples of the merchandise were displayed on those wooden hat stands shaped like giant toadstools. He'd say to the receptionist, "I wanna buy some hats for da little woman." The receptionist would buzz open the door to the other room, revealing, for just a few seconds, a bunch of guys in their shirtsleeves with their ears bent into telephones as they furiously scribbled down numbers.

During the war, the streets were lined with flags. The city was full of signs too—different ones every week, it seemed. HELP WANTED, SCRAP DRIVE THIS TUESDAY, BUY VICTORY BONDS, PERMANENT WAVES AT HOME. Women drove hacks and assembled parts for ack-ack guns. Movie marquees changed every other day. Newsies struggled to hold bigger and bigger bundles of papers under one arm as they waved a sample in the air with their other one. Every Joe and Jill appeared to be making good money, though rationing put a different complexion on how people spent the stuff in their pockets. Things that used to be made of metal, certain pieces of furniture for example, were being made out of wood. Old iceboxes with wooden doors fought back against Frigidaires made of steel. No new automobiles were manufactured and many of the ones still on the road started to look a little shabby and more or less alike. Pete Sells would have hated that.

Cynthia McConnell:

The only thing deader than a dead person, it seems, is a Montreal nightclub first thing in the morning in that brief period when the last customers have gone and none of the cleaning staff has yet woken up. Only a single light was on in the dining lounge, right above the table where Jim Joseph was sitting alone. On the opposite side of the room an unmarked door opened, letting in a rectangle of yellow light, and a male figure entered with a slow gait. I remembered Pete once overhearing something Jim said to Pete about the Carpenter. It was along the lines of this: "And these French-Canadians, you know, they're not *big* people. Smaller than us, most of them. Slightly built, not usually very tall. But Charpentier is huge. High and wide, massive arms, giant hands, but with big rolls of fat. He's heavy. One day he'll be so fat you might call him obese." That day had obviously arrived for the man whose name Pete always pronounced "Sharpen Tear."

Only the Carpenter's feet looked small. He wore beautiful handmade shoes, pointy shoes, not brogans. They gave him the appearance of a zoo animal, a small cousin of the hippopotamus perhaps, but a hippo wearing ballet slippers, which made a slight flapping sound with each step he took. When he arrived at the table he picked up two of the wooden chairs, put them side by side and sat down on both of them at once. Such was his girth that only his belly touched the table. The two men started to talk.

"Let me tell you of my troubles first so that you can then reply to me with yours."

Jim, taking off his hat, sat opposite, prepared to listen.

"Montreal is still full of visitors but not all of them are of the same kind as before. Soldiers and sailors. Airmen too. You have seen them already? They are everywhere. You notice that you do not hear them speaking French. *Des maudits Anglais*, most of them are. You understand this is not something I say to insult you, my friend; it is just how we say what we say. These people are young, maybe too young. In general, they are not gamblers, no. Instead they enjoy to dance and to make their eyes at the girls. Organizations, some English churches and non-religious *bienfaisants*, arrange big events for them in ballrooms and places like that all over the city. It is bad for my business. I have brought swing orchestras to the club, but the floor as you see is not big enough as it needs to be for these groups. They are not champagne buyers either." The big man chuckled at this. "Because they are English they drink *bière brune* and *bière blonde*, both. Sometimes two soldiers will make fists at each other. Sometimes their companions will join them in what happens next."

He paused and smiled a little. His tone changed.

"*C'est pas bien grave.* It is no big deal."

The two men talked until the earliest employees began

arriving and switched on more lights. The Carpenter quickly advanced to the next item on his agenda before the room became too busy for confidential topics.

"I am always happy to hear news of you, but some of the news I hear is not good. I am sorry things are going bad for you. Maybe I can do something to help."

"Thanks. You've done a lot for me already over the years. I like to think it has benefitted us both. But if you're suggesting what I think you might be, I've got enough dough to keep me going okay, though I'm glad to know I could borrow from you if I ever needed to."

"No, it's not that. Though it could be that if you were ever…" He decided against the last word. "What I mean is that I hear things all the time from men everywhere—Montreal, New York, Boston, Toronto, Detroit, Buffalo, Cleveland, Philadelphia, Miami. All over. People come to me at night and I help them, introduce them to people, maybe fix things that have broke. During the day I am nothing, nothing but a frog. I can do nothing on my own, or very little."

By the look on his face, Jim had obviously never heard him say such things before. He seemed a little embarrassed and for a few seconds he directed his eyes to the table top.

"But then it gets dark, as it always does, and then I become *le caïd de la nuit*." The big man's eyes suddenly opened wide, but otherwise his face said nothing.

Jim thought for a minute. "Are you offering me a job?"

"I am asking you to become a partner, an associate, a colleague, however you wish to say it."

"Despite what I said a moment ago, I don't have money to invest in anything else."

"You don't need to invest. Just join me."

"What would you need me for?"

The heavy man was aware that the time for candid talk was about to be ruined by the encroaching daylight. He must have felt as though he was about to lose his magical powers, like some character in a fairy tale. He spoke quickly.

"What the war *is* doing is making those who have houses of their own a lot of money."

Jim knew at once what he was talking about; they weren't discussing the real estate business. They went on a few minutes longer before Jim picked up his fedora from the table, and it struck me that I was being naive. They were talking about, well, bordellos. I wasn't necessarily shocked by the subject. When I was a young teenager a girlfriend and I would go to the Triangle (during the day of course) and look at people's homes that had small metal plaques next to the front doors that said "Private Residence." These signs were intended to prevent misunderstandings when men, probably men who had had too much to drink, sometimes mistook one dwelling for another and upset honest homeowners. And we giggled behind our hands at all the naughtiness. And then I thought of Hedy's life as a girl or young woman and suddenly I felt sad.

Jim had departed after trusting his fingers to the crushing folds of the Carpenter's huge bear paw.

This might be interesting.

So I began imitating one of those girl reporters in the movies. I don't know how long I was on the case, as those sob-sister characters say. Deceased Americans no longer have a concept of time that can be broken into hours, days, weeks, months, and years. Time is no longer artificially discontinuous; rather, it seems as though it's eternal and indivisible. I'm a quick study, just as I used to be at the Academy, winning many of the medals in various grades, and I soon figured out what Jim Joseph was doing as I followed him around.

By overhearing conversations I discovered that the Carpenter was himself an employee of some higher-up somebody known as the edge man. I never learned how that term came about. Most everybody in the circles I was studying probably lived on the edge, out of fear of being arrested for some crime, but the phrase wasn't applied to them. The edge man seemed to be the chairman of the board and the Carpenter (maybe there were others; there probably were) was like the office manager in the company, the managing partner in a law firm, or a top sergeant in the army. He kept things in running order for the benefit of the men above him who were far more powerful and who took home most of the money.

Jim seemed to have become the Carpenter's own subordinate, responsible for houses of prostitution—not everybody's, of course, but many of them. People didn't care to be identified with them too closely, for who would want to be known that way? So they paid some sort of regular fee to Monsieur Sharpen Tear, who then presumably gave a piece of it to Mr. Joseph to prevent problems from arising or to handle those that did. There must have been some reason why he chose an American to do this rather than a Montrealer who knew his way round the city and its workings. Perhaps Montreal people were more frightened of American gangsters than of their own.

Prostitution was a profession rich in tradition, and you wouldn't believe what went on inside. One day, just out of curiosity, I was floating up and down above the aisles of the Dupuis Frères department store on St. Catherine Street when my eye caught the latest thing in women's bathing suits. In any other culture it would have been called a dress, not a bathing suit, as it covered up most everything. A sign said proudly that the item was *"Approuvé par la Ligue catholique féminine."* What brothel girls wore used only a quarter as much material—when they were in the sitting room, I mean, for they wore nothing when upstairs in their rooms except maybe an open flimsy dressing gown part of the time. How could a city so conservative also be one in which the nightclubs stayed open until it was no longer night at all and the customers staggered home to their beds, sleeping until everything was jumping once again, only to begin a new cycle?

The most famous house of prostitution was at 312 Ontario Street. It was widely believed that a man had only to mutter three-twelve to a cab driver, with no further instruction, though this may be folklore. The other houses weren't famous landmarks. They didn't have to be because they were so numerous. I'm not talking about the girls who worked in some of the bars west of Bleury in the St. George district or around Windsor Station, but Bleury seemed to be the western boundary of the red-light district, just as St. Denis was on the east. North to south, the area stretched from Sherbrooke all the way down to Craig Street. An immense piece of the city, but the houses were scattered about, hidden among normal residences that were themselves sprinkled between commercial buildings.

This intrepid girl reporter picked up the scent of Mr. Joseph very early one morning. The subject was heading toward Cadieux Street. By tradition Cadieux was a street where Jewish families lived. From conversations I've overheard it once produced a number of famous Jewish gangsters and prize fighters. Many old people still called it Cadieux, and parts of it, I think, continue to bear that name, though it had been given a new one—de Bullion—in the late twenties to satisfy residents who wanted it free of its reputation for vice. De Bullion ran north from Sherbrooke and was the old red-light district before the people who were never true gentlemen in any sense nevertheless struck a gentlemen's agreement and the vice map got reorganized. Would the Carpenter have been involved in this?

Jim climbed the steps of one of the houses and pulled the bell cord. The madam herself answered.

"Good morning, Mrs. Henderson."

She answers civilly if not politely in a very heavy French accent. Madams were usually French Canadians (though I saw one who was a White Russian exile). They often went by English names (though Mrs. Henderson is likely not the only name she employs), not only to disguise their identity but also to win the confidence of the English-speaking customers. By contrast, while traditionally most of the prostitutes were French, there is a measurable minority who are English. In order to fit in, they operated under French names. There were Fleurettes and Huguettes galore. Those who wished to sound exotic might even choose Véronique or Kiki or Fifi. During prescribed periods of politically mandated vice raids, some of the girls who ended up in Sessions Court were sent to the Fullum Street lock-ups. In the artificially produced confusion some English girls were inevitably sent to the Catholic jail and some French ones to the Protestant jail. This was another of the little mishaps that the Carpenter's man had to straighten out. I wondered what would happen in the rare case of a French Protestant with an English name or an Irish Catholic girl with a French one? I guess she would have been counted as ambidextrous, so to speak. (Ambidextrous is a word I've always liked—I like how it sounds—but haven't ever before had the right opportunity to use it in a sentence.)

Edwin Staffel:

I managed to find work on the copy desk of the *Register*, but only four shifts a week, and a number of the other staff resented me for getting even that, since I was a *State Journal* alumnus and, what's more, a former hanger-on of Jim, whom McConnell openly despised and was constantly working to help bring down. Maybe they hired me to be a kind of stoolie, I'm not sure. It didn't matter because I felt sure I would soon be drafted.

Every now and then I'd see Kasdan on the street, hurrying along, looking worried. But then he was one of those people who had that kind of face, as though he was always about to inform you that your mother had just died. I knew Jim was up north but I heard nothing from him. Even gossip was scarce. I knew he must have been sneaking back, because more trouble was brewing.

First the US Navy made the Triangle district strictly off-limits to sailors and marines. Officially this was to eliminate prostitution there and thus venereal disease, but I can't have been the only one who suspected McConnell and Metzger were behind the ban. In a short time, the army followed suit.

Soon the Paddock Club was closed for good, just as the Roosevelt had been. The city government imposed a curfew on bars and clubs generally. And then there was the draft, which took off the streets not only thousands of young men not employed in war-related jobs but also its share of low-lifes as well. Such factors combined to make a pretty dull city for those who were accustomed to believing it otherwise.

Cynthia McConnell:

From time to time the newspapers published lurid stories about the girls, as even those well along in adulthood are always called. Occasionally they were depicted as blight on the city's respectable middle class of Montreal *Gazette* subscribers. Almost all such exposés told of girls, in these cases genuine girls, from some remote and wretched place with a name such as Sainte-Euphémie or Lac-Saguay who came to Montreal to help support their families by working as *servantes de maison* for perhaps eight dollars a week. In many articles of this type, particularly those in the *Herald*, which crammed as much sex and crime as possible into its tabloid pages, the girls had been tricked into accepting jobs that did not exist and so were lured into houses of a different kind than they had been expecting. Put another away, they had hoped to be downstairs domestics but had become upstairs inmates instead.

I watched as Jim and the madam had their regular early-morning meeting—the earlier the better, because then there were no customers in the building and probably no police anywhere nearby, unless they were there for some other purpose. Some houses were larger and fancier, many smaller and worse. Mrs. Henderson's represented the middle ground. She did not live on the premises.

For that, there was a so-called housekeeper whose role, as I think back, was in some respects not terribly different from that of our housemother at school, though her chores were different. On a cord around her waist Mrs. Henderson wore a ring of keys and also a paper-punch to punch a girl's ticket each time she had a customer. At any one time, there may have been six or eight or even ten girls on the job, for the old house had many rooms. Barring some special arrangement for special services, the fee was five dollars, of which the girl got two. That likely means as much as seventy-five dollars a week take-home pay, though some of that, in certain cases, went to purchase morphine or hop. (Memory takes me back to Pete and his nightstand.)

Jim and Mrs. Henderson went over the grosses and nets, figuring in Mrs. H's compensation and that of the housekeeper, whose duties included instructing new employees in what they had to do to avoid the Hôpital de la Miséricorde, which ran the city's first maternity ward, and so on. Jim collected the take and dispensed the disbursements, departing with a small valise of cash, out of which the money would flow upward into unknown hands. The rent, for example, was two hundred dollars a month, payable in banknotes to whatever name the owner was using at the moment, based on how recently he had redeeded the property to himself under yet another new identity. This owner may have done some recruiting and probably also supplied the drugs. I suspect that Jim assumed that this mysterious figure owned several such establishments and believed he must be, like himself, a friend of the Carpenter whom the Carpenter had rescued from some huge failure in life—in somewhat the same sense that an Henriette or a Thérèse has been rescued from Sainte-Euphémie.

Edwin Staffel:

I got drafted. There was no way to get a fix in. Among those sitting on the local Selective Service board were McConnell's son, himself scandalously still of military age, one of the shysters in Metzger's law firm, and various bankers and similar Parthenoners. I felt as though I'd been captured, not by the enemy but by my own people, and was being, at best, sent into exile—banished and vanished, outlawed.

Before my fourth month in uniform I got word that my wife was expecting. Except for letters and snapshots, I was out of touch with home, and everyone and everything around me kept me separated from what my life had been up to that point. I felt as though my life was coming to an end, the life I had known, but from time to time my mind would fix on Jim Joseph and what he must be going through. In religion we shared the same heaven but on earth had different hells.

Cynthia McConnell:

I must say that my French is getting better quickly as I flit about by day and by night. In retrospect, I'm glad to have had those three years of Miss McNally at the Academy interspersed with periods of travel with Mother. Still, I'm constantly—what's the English word I'm searching for this time?—flummoxed by Montreal's idioms and peculiarities. For example, a *tabagie* is obviously a business that began life as a smoke shop but has become a newsstand, confectionery and stationer's, a dealer in soda pop, toiletries, sandwiches and who knows what else, all rolled into one. As far as I can determine, the locations where such places are to be found, as well as their inventory and hours of operation, are identical to those of a *dépanneur*, which in France, I think, alludes to assistance for automobiles that have broken down.

Like me, Montreal grew up where it did, all by itself and without close parental supervision. It had only an absent mother and a strict but disinterested father who wanted only to make money and more money. Only the church could attend to its well-being. This is why so many people find the city fascinating: it is rigid and risqué all at once.

Edwin Staffel:

Somewhere in France, as the censors order the papers to explain and the newsreels like to say. That's the term. Well, I was certainly somewhere in France all right, but the officers told us nothing if they could avoid it. When everything was quiet, the way it sometimes got, even when it was spookily quiet, I thought of my wife and the baby, but every now and then I thought of Pete Sells, too, so far away, such old news, so very dead. Was his situation over here in 1917 any different from what was happening right now? Not different enough to make him what he became. He was a violent man. He had been a violent boy, probably a violent toddler before that, even a violent baby in his crib—but who can say? The army probably didn't have to teach him much. He already liked killing. He was a natural. I wondered if Jim thought about him too and blamed him, as he had every right to do.

Cynthia McConnell:

Monday is wash day, and backyards and balconies are festooned with laundry. In many of those streets lined with row houses, the kind you enter via spiral iron staircases out front, boys are shooting marbles or playing a sort of broomstick hockey, when they're not teasing girls. Other boys ("good boys") collect for the latest salvage drive: worn-out rubber tires, scrap metal of all sorts, almost anything made of leather, whatever helps the war effort. Icemen, milkmen, coal men and grocers make their deliveries. Those with trucks are conscious of gasoline rationing and the impossibility of getting new tires; those with horse-drawn wagons know that they won't be able to get the poor old creatures reshod. In those parts of the city where life has always been hard and shabby, it is harder and shabbier still—rationing, blackout drills, scrimping and saving, anger and fear. But for all that people are getting by somehow. Most everyone who isn't Jewish attends church incessantly, but even their Sunday best no longer looks so good.

And yet there's probably more money circulating than ever before, what with all the factories, foundries, railroads and the like giving the war their undivided attention. There are so many people working, flowing in from other parts of the country, that apartments are scarce and, when found, overcrowded. With so much money being paid out, nightlife has continued to boom—that is, once that business, too, has, as the men who run St. James Street say, retooled for wartime production.

My sense is that relations between the English and the French are about to boil over. I hear the bubbling and see the lid of the pot rise and fall, gently but ominously. A poster with the message *Enrôlons-nous* is pasted on a dirty brick wall. Next to it some vandal has painted À *bas la conscription!* in enormous red letters. The prime minister, that strange little round man, first promised not to draft men to go overseas but has had to do so anyway. He's come to that conclusion agonizingly through a series of frustrating stages that ended in a national referendum. No need to guess which side won. The English boys are signing up enthusiastically, to have adventure or to defend the Empire or both. The French have no desire to fight for England. A great number simply abstain, while some join up claiming they will be fighting for France.

The whole business is heated and confusing to say the least. For instance, despite its name, the *Ligue pour la défense du Canada* is an anti-war group, not pro-war. At one huge rally it organized, all foreigners were denounced, the British flag was burned and the crowd sang "Ô Canada." In the end, the rally became a riot and one group invaded a bordello on Ontario Street, frightening the staff and patrons and smashing all the furniture. I knew who would be responsible for sorting out that particular mess the next morning.

And sure enough tomorrow came right on time.

Edwin Staffel:

Some guys, even the ones you'd least expect to, kept diaries. In normal circumstances, I myself might have taken up the habit. But right then our existence was too dull to record except when it wasn't, and then we were busy trying to stay alive. But everybody looked forward to mail call, not knowing when the next one might be, much less where. The letters came in the wrong order, so I would learn that the baby "is completely recovered" only to find out weeks later what he had been sick with. Often at night I took out the snapshots. One of them had been taken by a street photographer (I was told there were a number of these fellows). I studied my dear wife's face and I looked at the two buildings in the background, trying to identify the spot where the picture had been taken. But I couldn't figure it out, and this worried me.

Allan Ostermeyer:

Year of wonders, 1944.

Harry Ship, the respected and affable gambling impresario, has hired Frank Sinatra—Frank Sinatra!—to perform at his supper club on Stanley Street; the lineup outside must account for half of the teenage girls in Montreal, or half of the English ones anyway.

A tall blonde woman, Willis Marie Van Schaack from Minneapolis, infuriates the clergy and many others but endears herself to nearly everyone else the moment she begins performing at the Gayety Theatre. Her stage name is Lili St. Cyr. A wise-cracking dot-dot-dot columnist in the *Herald* likes referring to her as an ecdysiast, which is a word made from a botanical term, referring to a flower that slowly loses its petals one at a time—until there are none.

When King George and Queen Elizabeth visited Canada in 1939, the mayor stood with them on the balcony of the Windsor Hotel. Surveying the excited mass of people down below, he said to the monarch, "You know, Your

Majesty, some of these cheers are for you also." That's just the way he is: big-hearted and doughy, a lover of crowds, and not always careful with his remarks the way most politicians are. Only a few months before the royal visit he shocked virtually everyone by saying that once the war reaches Britain and Canada "the sympathy of French Canadians in Quebec" will be with the Italian fascists, because the two peoples share a Latin temperament. But then people have often called him *l'Imprévisible*. The following year, the unpredictable one was arrested right outside city hall for opposing conscription, and sent to a prison camp in Ontario.

In July, General de Gaulle stood on that same balcony, praising the Canadian troops who were among the first to disembark in *"ma, je devrais dire notre, chère Normandie"* barely a month earlier. This was no casual remark. Surveys the past few years showed that sentiment among French-speaking people in Quebec has generally been pro-Vichy, aligned with the Nazis, rather than the Free French, the government-in-exile that de Gaulle ran from London. Now that the tide of war had turned, he was here to thank those who supported him and to try to win back some of those who did not. *"Vive le Canada!"* he shouted. The crowd answered, *"Vive de Gaulle! Vive le Canada! Vive la France!"*

Another sign of things returning to the way they once were: Mayor Houde was released and at the first opportunity got himself elected again—for the fourth time. His sometime nemesis Maurice Duplessis, tossed out of office as premier of the province shortly after the war began, was also re-elected. He and his Union Nationale party returned to power with all their strict Catholic turn of mind not just restored but, you might say, fortified. He is a stern-looking rectangular gentleman with thick black hair plastered down, a little moustache, very strong vocal chords, and a neck that seems to strain at his shirt collar, which is heavily starched, as are his views on life.

Cynthia McConnell:

The returning soldiers step off the trains at Windsor Station and Bonaventure Station, the same places from which they departed. Premier Duplessis doesn't care for what goes on in Montreal by night. His political strength lies with rural and small-town people, the more devout the better. As for crime, he opposes it only on moral grounds, not on economic ones, and in this matter swims in the same stream as the municipal government. Night-clubs and such are closed on the Sabbath but reopen with a bang at 12:01 a.m. on Mondays and are instantly crowded. Vice raids are held by appointment. The police shut down a place by padlocking an interior door, to a storage room for instance, or even a false door that leads nowhere at all; business proceeds as usual as though nothing has happened, for the customary payments have been made and small fines paid. Jim Joseph is occasionally sent to observe the proceedings in court and to give someone a lift home. Looking at what he has become, it is difficult to fully appreciate the world he had made for himself back in the United States. What he was in his salad days gave no hint that his status could ever be reduced to that of a mere handyman, which is what he has become. He is the Carpenter's servant.

The Carpenter made more money than usual during the war, not by supplying the troops, the way the St. James Street people do, but by supplying diverted gasoline and chocolate and other rationed or unobtainable goods to people he knew on the home front. He had quite a little network.

Jim has been seconded once or twice to deliver *matériel* to the troops—the soldiers of the night, one might call them. He has returned to the place where more or less he began, driving a truck with a cargo hidden under a black tarpaulin. He seems to feel no nostalgia, though his employer does. "The first money I ever made," the Carpenter tells him one evening, "when I was just a kid, was driving a truck full of Christmas trees down to New York. The village where I'm from, you've never heard of it, did a good business in the Christmas trees every year. The New Yorkers with money, they liked the taller Quebec trees better than they liked the trees from New England, but there were problems with taking what they called products of the forest over the border without spending money and following rules." He smiles at the recollection.

"The people around there were convinced by friends of mine—well, they gave their trees to us, you see, and we sold them in the parks and the squares in New York until the cops would chase us away, and then we would pick some other spot. And so on, load after load. This sounds a small potato as you would say, but believe me it was a swell set-up."

Allan Ostermeyer:

The statement that Montreal was a divided city is taken to refer to its two main languages, but it was divided in another way as well, between the day people and the night people, regardless of which language they grew up speaking. Shortly after the end of the Second World War, there was a billboard on the slope of the mountain that gives Montreal its name. When one day it advertised a brand of soap, the result was rhetorical pandemonium, for the ad, intended to emphasize the soap's gentle nature, depicted a naked baby. Untold thousands of nameless citizens cried out in protest. They were encouraged to do so by civic politicians, members of the clergy both Catholic and Protestant, and newspaper editorial writers of the sort who point with pride on Monday, Wednesday, and Friday but view with alarm on Tuesday, Thursday, and Saturday (for Canada, and Quebec especially, had no newspapers on Sunday, the Lord's day).

In a country where gambling was illegal in all its forms, even bingo for nickels and dimes, or possession of an Irish Sweepstakes ticket sold to help alleviate the suffering of the poor, here stood its largest city where gambling took in a hundred million dollars a year (in 1940s dollars). Montreal was a joint venture of criminality, authority and government.

On a per capita basis, Montreal in those days had more gamblers than Chicago, Miami, or New Orleans. As for prostitutes of all classes, from the fifty-cent-girls to the fifty-buck ladies, it was impossible to find an accurate tally because they came and went, as did the names they used. Ten thousand was often proposed as a total. One year, the winner of the Miss Montreal beauty pageant was revealed as having a thick morality file at police headquarters. Looking back, surely someone could have predicted that.

Cynthia McConnell:

The government and the church hate communists. Hate them and fear them. Like other more orthodox businessmen, the Carpenter hates them too, but mostly in the abstract. I suppose this is because communists aren't usually gamblers or even serious drinkers, though there are, apparently, people called "nightclub communists," as certain conservatives call well-off, socially prominent liberals. I'm not sure that the adjective part of the phrase ever applied to that doctor named Bethune, a surgeon at the Hôpital du Sacré-Cœur. He was an actual member of the Communist Party and died in 1939 helping wounded Chinese soldiers who were fighting Japan. Because of his politics rather than his good works, his memory is despised by the sort of Montrealers who read the *Gazette*.

There are some things at which I can only guess. For example, the Carpenter has evidently discovered an additional way of making money in this crazy world of 1945. There is much talk of communists infiltrating unions. Father didn't care much for unions either, but he dealt with them and for the most part kept the peace. This was in contrast to Pig Iron who, I'm told, had to carry a revolver in his last years and thought "Wobbly" was the worst epithet he could ever hurl at another person. Well, darned if it isn't *plus* ça *change plus c'est pareil* all over again, as some industrialists and financiers, I don't know who exactly, but St. James Street people I presume, appear to have contracted with the Carpenter to break up certain unions by whatever means necessary.

Whether or not these unions are run by real communists I have no idea, but I take it that such an accusation is useful in keeping the authorities from meddling too much in how the union members are dealt with. The Carpenter has assembled—what would you call it? A team? A squad?—of burly fellows to disrupt union meetings and scatter the men walking picket lines. They are armed with such weapons as the fat end of a former billiard cue with little slits into which razor blades are inserted. From bits of conversation I pick up, I gather that Jim Joseph is not comfortable being asked to supervise these men. He doesn't mind finding them to hire or seeing that they get paid. It is the violence that disturbs him. These must seem to him like jobs for Pete. Getting de Bullion Street girls out of jail, or rushing one to the hospital when she has had too many drugs—that's one thing, but the violence is something else entirely.

Obviously, the Carpenter has excellent intuition. He may move as slowly as an elephant but he thinks quickly, like a cat. I hear him trying to put Jim more at ease by explaining how, when the communists are driven out, there will be an opening for the pair of them and their friends to take over a union or two themselves. "There is going to be much money in unions," he says. "The manager of the business of the union is in a good situation. You sit in your office and things come to you."

Allan Ostermeyer:

The city's criminal life was like a set of nesting bowls, each one fitting neatly inside the next. Joseph had been reduced to working for Charpentier, but Charpentier had bosses of his own keeping him in his place.

The bag man was the person in charge of collecting what you might call taxes and fees from everybody on the one side and distributing it as retainers and dividends to the pols and cops on the other. The job often involved negotiation. The bag man went by the name Harry Davis, though nobody seemed to know what his real name was. He was a Romanian Jew, a short fellow with a prominent nose and a spoon-shaped chin, who turned up as a hard-working gambler when both he and the century were in their early twenties. He was no mathematical genius like Harry Ship, another prominent man in the field, but by the sweat of his brow and the nimbleness of his fingers, he prospered. By the turn of the decade he and a man named Max Shapiro (and there were no doubt other partners as well) owned a full-service gaming establishment at 1224 St. Catherine that was acknowledged as the city's most lucrative. Later Davis transformed what once had been a blind pig on St. Lawrence into a cabaret called the Frolics. Post-Harry, the place would have other names, one after another, until it deteriorated to the point where it became an art gallery. When Harry ran it, it was the top spot where gangsters of all religions and national origins could sit back and relax.

Davis was a public gangster, as many were in that era, but he was a private crook as well, deeply involved in activities far more illegal than gambling. In 1930, as later testimony tells us, Harry and a fellow Romanian named Charlie Feigenbaum entered into an agreement with a New Yorker, Pincus Brecher, to supply narcotics they would smuggle from Europe aboard ships bound for the port of Montreal, hidden in rolls of silk and other fabrics supposedly intended for the garment trade. Their job was to send it over the border into the hands of Brecher, who was working for one Louis Buchalter, better known as Louis Lepke of Murder Incorporated. Lepke, incidentally, was the person whose pioneering work in the field of strike-breaking had given Charpentier the idea of branching out.

Eventually somebody squeaked or else just got lucky, it's tough to tell which. In any case, early in 1933 the mounted police arrested Feigenbaum for dope trafficking, but he got off by informing on Davis and was sentenced to only six months. Davis was arrested a short time later on charges that during the 1930 calendar year he had dealt 852 kilos of opium, morphine, and heroin. There was also an additional charge of "corrupting public officials" though in Montreal at that time such an act was as much a sport or a hobby as it was a crime.

Davis had a five-day trial and was sentenced to ten strokes of the lash and fourteen years in Saint-Vincent-de-Paul Penitentiary (he would serve only twelve). That was in October 1933. The following August, Feigenbaum was leaving his brother's house on Esplanade Avenue when three men pulled up in a Hudson sedan and fired six .45 calibre bullets into his head and torso. None of the assailants was ever identified except by winks, nods, and arched eyebrows.

With Davis tucked away in his cell, the city needed a new bag man. The fellow's name, though perhaps not the one he was christened with, was Eddy Baker, nicknamed the Kid. He died of natural causes (it happens) in the summer of 1945 just as Harry was about to be let out. The timing was fortuitous but the result dangerous. Harry's personality had undergone some changes while he was away and they weren't necessarily ones for the better. Back at his old haunt on St. Catherine he raised everybody's mandatory contributions to twenty percent and generally became more of a dictator and less of a mediator, allowing Charpentier to increase his own station in life by gobbling up even more of the latter function.

Davis didn't like it that a French Canadian was getting too big, to say nothing of the Italians, the ones who finally got control, trampling the crops he had tended for so long. His newly acquired arrogance, probably the manifestation of his need to make up for time lost in prison, cost him the friendship, and worse, the loyalty, of many of his fellow Jews.

Davis issued an edict that no one would enter the gambling business without his approval. A man called Joe Miller (real name: Louis Bercovitch) asked for such permission but was refused. Davis got word that the rejected petitioner was going to hire a killer, but in the end Miller did the job himself, outside Harry's premises on a July afternoon. The year was 1946. Everybody in Montreal felt the shock waves.

The death of Harry Davis was an earth-shaking event. It not only rattled the chandeliers and wrecked the furniture but also changed the pattern of daily life from that point forward. I don't mean to say that Davis was a beloved local resident. He didn't have quite the easy charm of Harry Ship, at least not after his prison experiences. But everybody who wasn't afraid to know him, knew him. The way he was shot down in his early forties, in the street outside his casino, in broad daylight, as though his murder were a sporting event or some other public spectacle, made the city roil.

One of the consequences, one of the minor ones as far as Montrealers were concerned, was that Jim Joseph decided to return home.

Edwin Staffel:

The paper couldn't very well refuse to give me my job back, not a guy who'd been wounded in the Battle of the Bulge. So I became the police and criminal court reporter. This was a far less interesting beat than it used to be, when Jim and Pete were running things and Nolte was the chief of police. The golden age of crime seemed to be over, yet a lot of meaty stuff happened while I was in the service, and I had to catch up. I read everything I could find and talked to everybody willing to make chin music with me. I also kept an ear peeled for news from Montreal, and turned up there twice very briefly in rare weeks when I had more than one day off.

What I saw up there was that Montreal too was winding down. There was not much action in town anymore, not like I remembered. Even the barboots, as they called the joints where the game is played, had been shoved to the outer edges. And the Italians had more or less taken over from the Jews and the others. There had always been links between Montreal and New York. Remember that old song: "I'm leavin' in the summer and I won't be back till fall / Goodbye Broadway, hello Montreal"? A little ditty like that can hint at an awful lot of truth. Montreal had descended into little more than a colony of New York.

Once the business died down, so, I understand, did Montreal itself. Thus began the sad and long drawn-out end of a once great civilization, the civilization of the night people.

I got in touch with Jim, who put me on to the big man himself. "It's okay. He's from back home. He's worked with me for years. We're very close." The Carpenter looked skeptical at first, for it was always wise to be skeptical, but he finally shrugged his acceptance of me. For yours truly, this was a proud moment. Jim had never spoken to me the way he had just spoken of me. Without using the actual word he was saying that he trusted me. That's something my colleagues at the paper wouldn't do, which is why I never told anybody where I was going when I left for a few days.

I was crammed into the rear seat like the weakest puppy in the basket. The car moved haltingly through the crowds around the old Bonsecours Market and came out at the other side of somewhere. It was entirely different down here, almost a separate city all its own, made of railroad tracks, steel sheds, warehouses, elevators, piers. The funnels of all the steamships are lined up like a city skyline. Thick crowds of working men wearing identical clothes. I just sat back and listened.

"He came up from the States in '49. The owners gave him their invitation. The sailors' union is an all Canadian thing, which is very unusual. The companies with the ships, Allan and the rest of them, think the union is communist. Maybe they are, I don't care. I don't watch their politic. I can make business with anyone. Uncle Louis thinks they are communists too. So the owners and him agree to, I think these are the words, drastic measures. This is who I want you to meet. Mister Drastic Measures. I think there will be some money there for us to make from this."

Later I found out that Uncle Louis meant Louis St. Laurent, the prime minister.

I had assumed that we were going to an office, but instead we pulled up at what looked to be a bonded warehouse. It was late autumn and the river had not yet frozen over, which it did for four or five months of the year. The boss of the new Canadian branch of the Seafarers' International was a big stocky man with a furrowed brow and a chin like the ace of clubs. He was well turned out, custom double-breasted suit, silk tie and a gold tie-clip, the initials HCB on his shirt cuff. He looked as though he had had a shave, a haircut and a manicure sometime in the previous two hours. But he was a thug. Later I heard stories, conflicting stories, true, about a murder rap in either LA or San Francisco. There were a lot of stories but not many real facts.

I knew Jim well enough that I could read his mind the way deaf people can read lips. He was saying to himself that he's sick, sick to death, sick down to his soul, of muscle work. For one thing, he isn't terribly good at it, for another it's contrary to the beliefs he'd grown up with, and what's more, I'm pretty sure, it reminds him, painfully, of Pete.

Allan Ostermeyer:

April 1951. Staffel had gone through a kind of hell himself trying to get a telephone number for wherever it was that Jim Joseph was living up there. After exhaustive effort, he managed to wriggle it out of Kasdan, the gloomy under-employed bookkeeper. Staffel didn't want to call from the newsroom, but waited until he got home. The news was that the Keafauver lynch mob had just released its report and that somewhere down in the pile of type was Jim's name. He was listed as a former bootlegger who had expanded his criminal activities after Repeal and had not only come to dominate a small region but was one of those who, by being subservient to a national network of crime overlords with connections in other countries, made the whole system work. The senators were giving him far too much credit.

The floor beneath him was beginning to sag, and Jim thought he had better return to his own turf—once again—to see what could be done. Charpentier, I believe, thought his protégé, or partner or whatever you choose to call him, was chickening out. Maybe there was some truth in that, though the ruinous national publicity in the US was certainly a serious blow and had to be confronted, not hidden from. In any case, Jim Joseph was probably getting out of his Canadian refuge at the right time. Nobody in Canada publicly made the connection between Charpentier and the new Canadian district of the US-based Seafarers' International Union run by the California goon. Charpentier was too careful to let that happen. But those in authority had begun to link the goon's name with Jim's.

Edwin Staffel:

However long I live, I'll always remember that scene I stumbled into one Thursday morning, like the clumsy, lucky fool that I am. Sure, Jim was not the big operator he had once been. His business assets had been whittled down to the Mount Royal building and the horse wire, and maybe some other things as well. But Canada, the place he had seen as so promising—it's probably not wrong to call it a place he loved—turned out to be less and less glamorous the more time he spent there, and he found himself little more than a hired hand, working for someone he had once respected and even idealized. We all thought we were seeing the decline and fall of Jim Joseph. But what we saw was only the first step. I was witness to the beginning of the real trouble when I turned the corner into Commerce Street on my way to get a sandwich at the Vets Cafe. Guys wearing those government suits (you can always spot them, they all look exactly alike) were hauling boxes of files out of the Mount Royal and loading them into a panel truck. I watched for a few minutes and then ran back to the paper, but not before Kasdan came out to the sidewalk. He always seemed nervous, but now he was in some state akin to shock. He was quivering. I asked him what was going on. He couldn't give me a straight answer but that was okay because I knew. This was the time of year when a new federal grand jury had been empanelled, and this particular jury leaked like a rusted pipe. The G-men were going after Jim for taxes.

Three days later my boss told me I couldn't cover the story, whatever it might turn out to be, because I had once been on Jim's payroll and couldn't be trusted to be impartial. Offended, I argued that I was on the crime beat and this was a supposed crime and that my knowing the defendant would give the coverage a certain depth that younger reporters (they were all younger than me by this point) could not offer. Even at the time, much less in calm retrospect, I knew that I was on the verge of being discharged. And yet for some reason I wasn't, but was told to go ahead. Still, I sensed that I would be under close scrutiny.

I have my clippings, brittle and jaundiced now. Would it sound like bragging if I quote my long-ago self? "Bankers, insurance executives, federal intelligence men, and throngs of other persons jammed the corridors of the federal building this morning awaiting the call before the panel. Representatives of virtually every bank in the city were on hand along with Internal Revenue agents and associates of Mr. Joseph."

Jim posted a $5,000 bond and—let me summarize— faced one of four opening moves in the chess game that a trial of that kind inevitably becomes. He could submit a motion for dismissal, submit a motion asking for a bill of particulars, plead guilty, or plead not guilty. The government was claiming he owed hundreds of thousands of dollars on past income from a variety of sources. There were five separate charges, one for each year from 1936 to 1940. Each carried a fine of $10,000 and a maximum of five years in prison. That's not counting the civil penalty, which would mean the payment of one-and-a-half times the amount of the back taxes at six percent interest compounded annually. He had chosen one of the sharpest lawyers in the city, evidently an old friend—because I remember how enthusiastically Jim had welcomed him to the Mount Royal's opening night and how he personally steered him by the elbow to the gaming rooms. The man was undoubtedly a more talented lawyer than he was a gambler. Jim pleaded guilty to the 1940 charge and, in what only an idiot would call a coincidence, the prosecution dropped the other four.

I was in the gallery two weeks later when the judge asked, "Defendant James Joseph, do you have anything to say as to why the judgment of this court should not now be pronounced?"

"No." Jim's voice was firm.

Whereupon the judge surprised everyone by giving Jim the maximum five-year sentence, specifying the federal pen in Atlanta.

From where I was sitting I could see only Jim's left side but I'll never forget the expression of shock and disbelief on his face or the sudden deflation of his posture. He recovered his composure almost at once, however, and then did a most unusual thing, one that was an even greater surprise to the audience than the sentencing had been. He walked over to the prosecutor and offered his hand for shaking and said a few words. Then he went to the bench and approached the judge, who paused a few seconds before taking Jim's mitt, as the two men exchanged what

I imagine were dry pleasantries. The strange courtesies completed, Jim walked calmly to the dock to be led away. The judge's eyeglasses had slipped down and he used the ring finger of his right hand to push them back up to the bridge of his nose as soon as the small talk concluded.

Jim was soon free on bail and given six weeks to get his affairs in order before surrendering to the federal marshal. He left by the side door and bundled himself into a sleek sedan with a couple of friends or colleagues I'd never seen before, and, whoosh, he was gone.

Everyone assumed that the matter ended right there. But a short time later Jim's legal squad (two additional lawyers had come aboard) filed a lengthy document with the court. It was a motion for a new trial, stating that the defendant had been betrayed by the judge after having been promised, through unnamed intermediaries, that in exchange for his guilty plea Jim would get off with a stiff fine and a long spell of probation. The motion, which ran to about twenty pages, included references to the "close and intimate friendship" the defendant and the judge had shared over the years. The judge stayed mum but the prosecutor filed what's called a resistant document, calling Jim's assertion untrue. Jim's lawyers replied in writing that they could produce witnesses attesting to the judge's conflict of interest.

Suffice it to say that the judge ordered a new trial. Jim declared himself happy to finally have a chance to defend himself in open court, and provoked loud legal howls from the prosecutor. In an unprecedented move, McConnell himself signed his name to a front-page editorial in the *Register* in which he came as close as possible to calling the judge a tool of the gangsters without actually being cited for contempt of court.

Editors and radio commentators across the country pounced on the story and suddenly Jim was a national figure. Metzger by now was retired from politics, but this meant he had much more free time to undermine Jim, using his friends in Washington to drum up an image of a criminal mastermind, dripping with evil and sucking the moral marrow from America's bones.

There was a different judge and a change of venue, and the entire circus, including two skeins of brand-new lawyers, began the process all over again. The government was still concerned with just the early and mid 1940s, partly because audits and investigations had lagged far behind during the war—it had been a golden age for tax cheats.

In time, some observers believed, the government would eventually lay charges for years later than 1946, though others felt that Jim's business was obviously being run so much more professionally by that time that the pickings would be thinner. In any case, there was no going back to the 1920s and 1930s; the statute of limitations had kicked in. Once again, McConnell took up his pen to write a front-page editorial: a new generation of gangsters, outsiders from Cleveland or Detroit perhaps, were sure to descend on the helpless city to fill the vacuum that would be left by Jim's imprisonment. They were sure to be men with even more murder in their hearts than those who had been associated with Jim Joseph in the past.

Allan Ostermeyer:

Long after being called to the bar so many years ago I found that the profession really didn't suit me. Later, I lived elsewhere, but after several other careers in sequence, resettled here for personal reasons. When I did so I was struck by the sheer abundance of lawyers. They seemed to outnumber even doctors. They were everywhere.

As my residence in this city grew by years and then by decades, I got to know many or most of these firms. Looking into the Jim Joseph story, I see how many lawyers he retained over the years. The total, if an accurate one could be drawn up, was astounding. What astounds me is the frequency with which the familiar names of the members of the local bar appear and reappear. Jim Joseph's troubles dragged on for so many years that he would find himself retaining the son, or even, in one the instance, the grandson, of someone who had represented him in his younger days. There was even one case in which he was defended by the offspring of someone who had been the prosecutor in one of his much earlier trials. How he must have sighed as he emptied his wealth into their green bags.

That's not to say that he failed to receive top-notch legal work, but after his first serious brush with the law over income taxes, his life was no longer that of an entrepreneurial free spirit but that of a full-time defendant. Two lines of action were intertwined. His legal people (in this instance, eight lawyers drawn from half a dozen firms) beat back the government's first campaign against him.

Their tactic was first to delay, then to delay some more, and then to seek a mistrial after showing that the judge had been an inveterate gambler who had frequented the Mount Royal Club, such testimony coming from a variety of sources, including past employees of said establishment, one of whom swore that the management let His Honor win at baccarat—repeatedly. That gave Jim's lawyers time to trump up, for use if necessary, a few highly dubious procedural errors on the government's side. The persecution resumed when prosecution got under way in another city. The new judge was bombarded with filings, dropped like so many propaganda leaflets over enemy territory, urging the troops to desert.

In the end, Jim's array of legal talent won the case after proving that during the period in question the defendant was deeply in debt, owing partly to his own huge gambling losses. So swore various dubious characters in the gaming fraternity. Therefore he couldn't possibly have had tax arrears so big as the enemy claimed. A certain percentage of the money located by the government in a series of safe deposit boxes at local banks was actually that of the absent Mrs. Joseph, as indicated by the fact that the boxes were registered in both names. The government mumbled about bringing her back to the United States to testify, or even of sending an official to Beirut to take a deposition from her, but these ideas came to nothing—of course. Yet the idea may have put a bug in the ear of another branch of the government.

Even before the relevant authorities could begin

building new evidence for a fresh fraud case covering a different set of tax years, there was rapping on the door of Jim's apartment. He answered the door barefoot and wearing a dressing gown. The immigration officer who arrested him as an illegal alien later testified that the vast apartment, once obviously so grand, was dishevelled and a little dirty, though he said it was hard to see the interior clearly, as the drapes were drawn—and appeared as though they had been for months or years—and the place was dark and dead-looking, except for one weak shaft of diagonal light from a small window. But this beam merely showcased the dust particles as they did their slow crazy dance around the place.

Cynthia McConnell:

Imagine a manhole cover. It starts to rattle a little bit. Finally it flies off, and Jim Joseph emerges from the sewer drain. *I come up from nothing and out of nowhere*, he thinks. He went through the old Eighth Ward elementary school where he got good grades in two subjects, math and metal shop. He helped the younger boys playing with marbles graduate to something better: shooting craps; it's like moving from short pants to trousers, he told them.

Pete was his best friend. He was skinny back then, but wiry, and much better than Jim was at jumping on the rear bumper of a streetcar and holding on while staying crouched down. It wasn't that they didn't want to pay the nickel, it was the excitement of not paying and still getting wherever they wanted to go—sometimes one of the stores on Commerce Street where they'd work as shoplifting partners. He was faster than Jim was—faster at grabbing what they wanted, much faster at running out with it. Jim's job was just diverting attention, though later he sent up a kind of fence network, shoplifting what a particular kid wanted and would pay half the store price for. Pete had a real knack for fixing automobiles. When Jim married his sister, it just seemed right for the two of them to be in some sort of auto business together. Everybody knows where they went from there.

Jim knew that Pete liked speed but until the war came along he didn't quite understand that, to him, speed was a part of the violence and vice versa. He wasn't patriotic about anything but himself, but you never saw anyone who enlisted quicker than he did. All young fellows, most of them anyway, dream about adventure, even long for it. But for Pete there was more than that in his mind. He went into the army a guy with axle grease under his fingernails. He came out knowing how to take apart a Lewis gun, clean it, and put it back together. I think he may never have forgotten not only the thrill but the sense of accomplishment as well.

Or something like that. I'm a ghost, not a gypsy mindreader. As Pete would have said, "This ain't no carnival sideshow."

Allan Ostermeyer:

Jim was still out on $3,000 bail when the government was set to commence its second tax fraud case against him. All those who disliked him, and that includes of course the clergy, the do-gooders, the spavined old Parthenon guys and the forces loyal to McConnell and his newspaper, said to themselves, "This will be the end of the bastard. Good riddance." Those on the opposite side of the issue sensed a government conspiracy against a poor individual citizen.

If a citizen is indeed what he was. The immigration authorities were claiming that his parents had arrived in this country in 1899. They had the passenger list of the vessel that brought his parents to New York for eventual dispersal across the country. It included, but didn't actually name, for as yet he had no name, the immigrants' infant child—whether male or female, wasn't specified. As there was and is no record of this baby having any siblings, the government was contending that Jim had been born in Lebanon. As there was no record of his ever having been naturalized as an American citizen, Jim was therefore an alien—and so required an alien identification card to enter the United States. Washington had proof that he had entered the United States from Canada at various times in the 1930s and 1940s without such a card, without any identification at all. Just how he did so, they couldn't say. During the war years, both American citizens and Canadians, as a special security measure, needed their respective passports to cross the border.

A day was set for an immigration hearing that would lead to Jim's deportation as an undesirable alien. But the state scuttled the date when Jim's lawyer (he had only one at the moment—cleverly so, perhaps) sought a postponement because of his own illness. The prosecutor demanded a doctor's statement describing the attorney's illness and indicating when he would be well enough to begin. By doing this, the government shot itself in the foot, delaying matters still more, as the physician, in fact several of them, were deposed. They seemed to have been chosen carefully with the intent of giving widely varying diagnoses and prognoses. After all that was settled and frustration started to wane, the immigration people asked that the hearing be postponed until the new trial for tax fraud was actually on the docket. Jim must have been smiling on the inside, knowing that old man Metzger, as he now was, an ancient dark angel sulking in his castle somewhere, was doubtless in a state of acute exasperation.

In time the whole affair came down to this: a jumble of extraordinary facts unknown to most people in town, even to some of those in the Lebanese community. Jim's father had perished suddenly just before the great influenza epidemic of 1918. By then he was a widower, his wife having died trying to have a second child. Jim's lawyer argued that the sketchy scribbled records from Ellis Island referred not to a living child but rather to the fact that the woman being interviewed for a brief moment was, very obviously, in the last stage of pregnancy. She had often told Jim the story of how scared she had been, separated from her husband and sent to the women's section by nurses who feared that she might give birth right on the spot. No one on duty, it seemed, spoke Arabic, and she spoke no English. Jim was born shortly afterwards, in a quarantine ward where some new arrivals were kept for a certain time to see whether they suffered from tuberculosis or some similar contagion. There must have been some variety of document laying out the unusual circumstances of his birth, but he had never seen it. Yet he was adamant that he had been born in New York, almost within sight of the Statue of Liberty, and that the family, once reunited, moved on to their final destination as soon as it was all right for him to travel. His mother frequently told him the story of trying to keep him quiet in his wicker baby basket as the train rattled through the foreign-seeming darkness, heading west.

The government responded that all this was poppycock. Somehow the prosecution produced another Lebanese woman who had been a passenger on the same ship. She testified that Mrs. Joseph was not pregnant during the passage, at least not in any way that was in the least visible, and that she did not act as though she were and said nothing about the subject to anyone. Making every possible allowance for whatever unusual circumstances attend this case, the prosecutor asked, why was there no New York State birth certificate? Why was there no such record, Jim's people shot back, not even a baptismal one, in the place where they contended he was born—Beirut?

The matter dragged on but often took odd turns, some

machines, a few from Detroit, a few others from Toledo or Cleveland or Albany, and so on. They arrived in crates by truck or by rail, marked as something else: electrical equipment, prayer books, and even—now this was irony—liquor. Jim dutifully paid the commission the Carpenter asked, which no doubt equalled what he received from the contraptions' actual owners. The lessors, you might say. At its zenith, the Joseph-Sells combination was said to have 374 one-armed bandits in the city and its environs.

One day the unthinkable happened. Bandits were installed in the billiard room of the Parthenon Club, a long row of them, though it was understood that in any place but a bar or nitery they would be housed in wooden cabinets that could be locked at certain hours. Nolte had come up with this so as to take a little edge off the opposition. But the city's defensive walls had been breached. The Metzgers of the world and all the interlocking worthies—the steel men and manufacturers, the investors, the bankers, the retail barons and the leading members of the bar (that left me out of course)—were at base no better than the Triangle's petty gamblers. The Parthenon crowd saw no change in their lives. The club would go on as it always had, with the members concocting their deals while those who served them drinks and meals high-hatted their fellow Negroes who did housekeeping work for seven bucks a week, plus room and board and Thursdays off. But for Jim Joseph, this expansion was close to a volcanic eruption. He knew where to go from there.

Cynthia McConnell:

Pete had a strange way of showing remorse.

Weeks passed. Father hadn't cut off my money yet and so I went to the house to get more clothes and things. Hedy was very helpful, as always, and I was sad to part from her. As for Father, he had learned of the Pete incident somehow, presumably from Jim Joseph, and he cornered me with accusations and insinuations. It was a long argument that I can't recall word for word. This is what death does to you: it robs you of the literal but heightens your understanding of the fundamentals. Time expands and contracts simultaneously while going on forever, continuously, without being artificially broken up into days, nights, weeks, months, years. The essence of our meeting was that I (and the world) would be lucky to be rid of a monster such as Pete and that I should move on with my life, perhaps even move far away.

But I stayed in town in a place I'd found, and one night Pete turned up at the door. He was alone but all jazzed up. I don't know what he'd been taking, but he couldn't stand still. He started yelling. He was talking wildly, ordering me to come back, pleading with me, following me from room to room with quick heavy steps, occasionally banging into some piece of furniture or accidently knocking over a lamp or some other object. I kept resisting him, moving as far away from him as I could, but that turned the accidental breakage into a violent ransacking. He yanked the telephone from its cord and threw it across of them hypothetical or theoretical or simply rhetorical, as can happen when opposing lawyers are turned loose. I think you will see why I abandoned the practice of law without ever neglecting my observation of its workings. The government continued to hound Jim Joseph for the rest of his life, dragging him into court even when he had become penniless and critically ill. Did he wonder why he was being punished? As far as I could see, Jim was the beneficiary of no forgiveness whatever, not in this town, at least not by those in authority. I was a lawyer, yes, but I wasn't one of them. I hardly need repeat that I was never a member of the Parthenon Club.

Edwin Staffel:

I spent all those years in the newspaper business, writing stories, editing stories, reading stories, only to realize now, at this late stage, that I have no story of my own. The news goes on and on, like a dripping faucet, and after a certain age you have to stop listening if you're to remain sane. You make do with obituaries, those of people you knew and places you once inhabited. With the steel mills virtually gone, the city I grew up in became a town I could scarcely recognize. Buildings were razed and people faded away. Metzger hung onto life like a lizard on a flat rock in the desert, but went eventually, of course. Clouse is gone too (heart attack) and of course Jim Joseph (penury, loneliness, despair, first one stroke and then another). A few young small-time punks notwithstanding, nobody ever replaced him; there wasn't enough money left in the city to make crime worthwhile. Many of those still alive packed up and left. I remember Kasdan's departure, for example; he moved somewhere in Florida. I run into a few individuals from the old days, but on such occasions I always come away wondering whether they will be around to read my own death notice. What will it say? Edwin Staffel, long-time newsman, succumbs. Keep it brief and punchy.

Allan Ostermeyer:

Whatever Montreal may have been in the 1930s and 1940s, the city is something else now. Staid and business-like and perhaps a little rundown. A city more of anger than of frivolity. I presumed that Charpentier (I didn't know his first name or names) was no longer living, but there was no death notice or obituary, just as there was no birth certificate for Jim Joseph. Every old telephone book in the public library had more Charpentiers than you could possibly imagine, but none of these directories for the relevant years, whether white pages or yellow pages, contained a listing for a nightclub called the Grotto. Retired reporters and police officers who might have been around in those days were either suspicious or genuinely ignorant.

One old timer put me on to another of the same vintage whom he thought could help. I rushed to see him.

He said he had once heard of someone who fit several of the Carpenter's particulars down to the last detail but had never actually seen him and, in any event, the subject's name was either Robicheau or Robicheaux. Was Charpentier an alias? It might have been. Or perhaps such a person simply never existed at all. I was wasting my time on the brittle yellow news of the previous generation rather than making a contribution to my own or preparing myself for the one that was growing up now, a process that always leaves one fearful and absolutely certain that the world is going to hell.

Cynthia McConnell:

Growing up, we read stories about historic ghosts who have haunted the same castles for hundreds of years. The truth is that we don't even know how long we exist in this faint carbon-paper copy of real life. We evaporate eventually to make way for others even though the room for us seems infinite. I don't believe we are born twice but it seems we can die a second time, as the ghost spirit is punctured like an automobile tire and the energy hisses out and leaves us flat—and gone.

Nolte, the handsome young policeman who eventually got to be the chief, became a different person from the one I first met at Passavant Hospital when I was volunteering there. He also seemed to be nearby during the times I was with Pete, and I presumed that Father had told him, ordered him, I guess, to keep an eye on me, not knowing what sort of trouble I might get into next. I had no way of understanding that, as time went on, he grew to hate me because I hadn't fallen in love with him as he had with me. Really, I had no idea. His emotions must have corroded his equilibrium. When he confronted me with his feelings, I was astonished. He became so angry with himself that his anger spilled out and splashed all over me, and the bullet tore me open. He stood looking down at me, still with his police pistol in his hand. He smoked a quick cigarette. And he left me there, stark dead. Pete was a bad man. It's stupid and careless to let a bad man seem exciting. But he wished me no harm. I was one of the few of whom this could be said. He would have protected me, the jerk. If only things had worked out differently.